First Edition.

Ebook ISBN: B0BCXT8467

Paperback ISBN: 9781916521131

Publisher: Dirty Talk Publishing

Editing: Mom Loves Books Editing and Proofreading

Cover Design: Maddison Cole

Formatting: Emma Luna at Moonlight Author Services

To everyone who decided Hoax needed a voice.
To all of those who struggle in the dark.
You're not alone.
There's always someone, somewhere who loves you.
Even if it's beyond the veil.

BLURB

Everyone has a story to tell. Even the dead.

Trapped in limbo between Hell and Earth, I've been dealt a fate worse than death. To witness the suffering of those I love, unable to communicate or help. Or am I? With the appearance of a demon I've yet to decide is foe or friend, I'm discovering my spirit isn't as useless as I'd previously thought. The odds are stacked against me, the possibility of holding Mania again a pipe dream, but one thing is for sure. My brothers and my girl need me, so this is not the time to give up.

As asked for by the readers, this novella is solely from Hoax's point of view. To avoid spoilers, I highly recommend for this book to be read after Kings of Madness - book two in the All My Pretty Psychos series. All of your unanswered questions await, and Hoax is ready to reveal the truth behind the story. #GiveHoaxAVoice.

AUTHOR NOTE

If you enjoy Hoax, please consider leaving a review on Amazon and Goodreads.

Reviews help authors get more recognition and promotion, and it's also helpful to get your feedback.

If you find any issues or grammatical issues in this book, please don't report them using Amazon's new feature.

Instead, contact me using the details at the back of this book, and I will ensure they get fixed straight away. Contacting me directly ensures it gets fixed quicker.

Please also remember that despite being a UK based author, this book is based in the US, and uses US English spellings.

HOAX

All My Pretty Psychos Book 2.5

MADDISON COLE

"*Thank you for showing me how to love.*"

Those were the last words Mania heard me say before I disappeared from her life. Not completely, and it's not like I was even fully a part of her life in the first place. Only in spirit. A useless entity that can't hold his girl, soothe her with his words, or protect her in the face of danger. Whether I found her or she found me, our paths were tied long before I died. She was meant to be mine. I don't need my memories to know that.

Lowering onto my hunches, I pretend to rest my back against a gravestone. A full moon hangs over the decrepit chapel opposite, dousing the rooftop in light and casting this side of the building in shadow. An iron cross stands on the tip of an arched doorway, spearing the perfect lunar sphere. Where my memories are hazy, my general knowledge seems to be intact, and it baffles me the lengths humans go to justify their decisions. They hunt the Mutes, cage and torture them merely for existing and then pray for forgiveness. Seems like a strange way to show faith but after seeing the pits of Hell, they're right to be fearful.

The howl of a coyote can be heard in the distance, breaking through an otherwise peaceful night, and my thoughts. Life as a spirit isn't all it's cracked up to be. Sure, I can walk through walls and I'm learning how to shift through space to appear elsewhere. But when time passes both too quickly and dreadfully slowly, an eternity of only watching others laugh and love seems like a punishment in itself. Maybe I used to be an asshole. Maybe I deserve it. At least now Mania has found Ghost, my soul can be at ease. A teeny tiny bit. I stood by watching them enter the abandoned church and hung back, deciding some things need to be private. The pair have a strained history to work out and honestly, I don't want to be around the inevitable fall out. Their relationship will get worse before it gets better, that's for sure.

"Hoax," a deep voice barks. It's been so long since I've been addressed, it takes me a moment to realize the voice wasn't in my head. Shooting upright, a figure leans against a statue of an angel across the graveyard. Most of his body and face are hidden in the shadows, except for the right side. Between his eye and the line of his beard, deep crevices mar his skin and glow from the molten lava flowing just beneath the surface. I recognize him as the guard from the gates of Hell. Asher.

"It's time to come with me," he tips his head into the light of the moon, peering over a pair of black specs. When I don't move, the demon smooths a hand over his combed hair and takes a step forward. There's a strange look in his eye, almost desperate but bored at the same time. "Don't make this harder than it has to be. We need to go. Now."

"Why?" I hedge, taking a measured step backwards through a gravestone. Images come flooding back of seeing myself mirrored in Christopher's creepy tank. Words can't describe how seeing yourself suspended in a tank filled with liquid feels, and when the machine was turned off...I don't even want to think about the consequences that lack of oxygen might have done to me. Perhaps I won't need to, if Asher's appearance is anything to go by. "Is my body...is it official? I'm dead?"

"I don't know about that. New orders came in and I'm here to retrieve you." I raise an eyebrow at Asher's vagueness, curious as to why he'd have been sent over all other demons.

"Got off guard duty at last," I challenge, no longer retreating. Peeling the specs off his face, the full force of Asher's malicious goldeneyes glare at me as a silent stand-off commences. Mania had told me that Asher was in the Devil's doghouse for abusing his power with the female prisoners. I may not have the whole story yet, but he doesn't need to know that.

Scampering feet near, presenting the coyote I most likely heard before. Pulling up short, he twitches his nose high in the air, detecting a shift in his surroundings. I cock my head, wondering just how much the animal can sense when a spirit and a demon are so close by. Pushing his hand against the angel statue, Asher sends a bolt of Hellfire through the stone, splintering it into pieces. The coyote is gone before the first chunk hits the ground and the look on Asher's face shows his patience has truly run out.

"Look, I get you have a job to do," I hold my hands up as if that would stop him from advancing. "But I can't leave her." My eyes flick towards the church, which I only now realize has been rather quiet. I'd been expecting a full-blown fight to break out the moment the door closed.

"Mania's nothing if not headstrong with an undisputable knack for bouncing back," Asher snorts. "She can always come visit you next time she dies." Unbeknownst to Asher, next time won't be a casual drop-in to Hell for her. It'll be final. Mania could end up in a cell, being eternally tortured for her sins as a human. I can't stand by and watch her suffer like that, especially when she hasn't had the chance to live a proper life up here. Slowly shaking my head, I take another step back towards the church. I can't let that be our story. I refuse to let that be our ending.

"Don't be stupid, Hoax. You can't resist the summons," Asher warns. He has yet to move after me though, preferring to remain by the broken statue.

"You don't understand. I'm not leaving her!" Anger ripples through the center of my soul, knotting itself with a fierce need to protect Mania. Fisting my hands, the feeling inside grows. Expanding and evolving into an emotion much more potent. Unhindered rage. For too long, I've been kept from those I know I'm supposed to love. In every trial they've had to face, I've been forced to watch as a bystander, unable to help. All because an asshole with an ego problem took my consciousness away from my body, leaving me in a state of limbo.

Crackling catches my ear through the swirl of sensation bubbling inside. Looking down past my black cargos and canvas shoes, the grass around my feet is turning black in the light of the moon. Not just black, but dying. Shifting my heel, the now-charred grass breaks off and drops into crisped remnants on the ground. I've seen grass like this before, outside the gates of Hell, but the circle around me would imply I did that. I did...something.

"Hoax," Asher's voice comes in warning again. His stance has shifted into defensive mode, his gold eyes trained on my fists. Bringing them up in front of my chest, each of my clenched hands is surrounded by a hazy, purple glow. I don't know what that means, but a slow smile spreads across my face. Oh, it's on. Lashing an arm out, the force of my blow shoots across the graveyard with a purple trail streaming behind. Landing in the middle of Asher's chest, he flies backward and skids into a marble headstone. Unlike me, he seems to have the ability of being present in the real world, not a wandering figment of imagination.

"You're making a mistake," he grumbles, pulling himself to his feet. Dusting off his leather demon attire, Asher plucks his glasses from the ground and places them over the inferno raging in his eyes. "I'm not the bad guy here."

"Anyone who tries to come between Mania and me is the bad guy," I spit. Pumping my fists in front of me in quick succession, Asher is able to dodge a few of my purple force fields, but not all. Pieces of his leather tunic disintegrate, showing the affect my blows are having against his skin. Or more rather, the chunks of flesh ripping away from his now exposed ribs. Holy shit. Lava drips from his exposed bones before the skin heals back over and Asher uses a gravestone to push himself upright.

"It's only going to become more volatile until you take your place in Hell. Your soul will tear itself apart at the seams until there's nothing left!" he bellows, stilling my movements. I peer at my hands, suddenly weary of the newfound power I thought was a gift. Flexing out my fingers, the purple glow dissipates and the ball of anger inside eases. This isn't me. From what I've seen, Ghost is the one in our group who acts first and damns the consequences. Moving back to his spot by the broken angel statue, Asher calls for a scepter to appear in his hand. "It's time you entered through the Hellfire. Receive your judgment."

"And if I don't?" I ask, keeping my distance. His eyes flare through the tint of the glasses, the lava in his cracked face pulsating.

"If you make me come back here again, I will take your judgment into my own hands. Mania won't even recognize the shell of a man left and you'll spend the rest of eternity wondering if she was really worth it." Wrong answer. Snapping my hands back into fists, accompanied by the flare of rage that fills my entire soul, I throw a punch into the air, directly parallel with Asher's chest. He can't avoid the blow, sailing backward with a hole speared through his chest before he even hits the ground.

Then, I turn and run into the church, disappearing through the closed door. It's probably archaic to think Asher can't follow me in here, but whether he can't or just didn't, I stand alone at the altar as the seconds tick by. Stupidly, as I wait, I realize I'm forcing my chest to heave up and down as if my heart was beating rapidly. Man, I hope I get to be alive again one day. Now I know Pyro's eternal flame could possibly bring me back from the dead, I'm craving it more and more with each passing day.

Time slips by and my anger fades to the point where I don't even recognize the man that was out in that graveyard. The thought of being ripped away from the world where Mania is stirred something so visceral in me, I'm fairly certain I wasn't capable of such emotion even when I was alive. I may not be any help wandering Earth as the invisible man, but it beats accepting my fate in Hell. Once I cross into the fires, there's no coming back.

Remembering the reason I was haunting the outside of this forgotten church, I go in search of Mania and Ghost. Walking through the walls, it becomes quickly apparent they're not on this level so I head down a pair of aged stone stairs. That's when I find Ghost, hiding in a crypt. Highlighted by the flickering candles mounted on each wall, he's sat against a tomb with his knees raised. Pressing his fingers together, the look of concentration etched into his face strikes me as odd.

"Hey man," I say, knowing full well he can't hear me. "Hard day?" I drop down beside him. "Yeah, me too. Some asshole just tried to take me back to Hell–" Ghost suddenly moves, crawling across the ground like an animal. I follow curiously until he stops in front of a bundle stuffed in a hole among the cracked stone blocks.

I hadn't even realized Mania was here, but I've now spotted the vibrant, red hair poking out from beneath two covers. She's huddled up in the same way I've seen her do at the various squatter's buildings she's been staying at lately. Usually her holey socks are poking out the end of the coat she uses as a blanket and her shivering has been uncontrollable. At last, she's finally warm and able to sleep deeply enough to not rouse when Ghost reaches out a hand and brushes the hair away from her forehead. His thumb lingers over the crack dividing the center of her skull before her face disappears into the covers.

A hint of jealousy hinders on the edge of my subconscious but I bat it away. I've felt enough new emotions for tonight. It's not Ghost's fault he is there with her, in the present, and able to touch her. I'm more frustrated by his nonchalant attitude when it's clearer than ever, all he wants to do is crawl into that hole and hold her. Shuffling back to the nearest wall, I leave them to their moment, wondering what it will take for Ghost to man up and admit his feelings. Or more worryingly, how severe the situation will have to be before he'll do so.

I stay the whole night, watching over Ghost and Mania. Right up until he mounts her on his MV Agusta motorbike and they ride towards the impending sunrise. It didn't feel right to keep trailing around after them, not when I've felt the distinctive loss of another that should have been with us.

Since the moment I saw Pyro leaning over my dead body in the bakery, I felt a bond to him. The way he held my hand, the way he cried searing tears for me. I didn't need to know him to see he loves those he considers worthy endlessly. A blessing and a fault as far as I'm concerned. He broke the day Mania was forced to lie about the love they shared, all to save my body from deteriorating any further. Something I've felt so thankful and guilty over, yet I haven't tried to check in on him. Since the eternal bond snapped, I've found I'm no longer tied to Mania, and have attempted to hone shifting through space between locations. It's a work in progress but I think I've almost got it sussed.

Closing my eyes, I visualize Pyro's face in the forefront of my mind. Flame red hair, scorching red eyes. Tattoos lining his skin, namely the winged skull in the center of his chest. The gentle look of understanding in his features and easy smile at the ready. But when I open my eyes, that's not the Pyro I find.

A defeated heap of skin and bones lies crumpled on the ground of a damp cell. His hair is barely crimson at this point, his eyes not even open. Scored lines slashed across his back drip with blood, the wounds the only things angry and red on him. I knew it'd be bad, but this is so much worse than I imagined. Thick bars block Pyro's exit from the hallway beyond, not that he's making any effort to escape. Shadows leer across the leaking stone, low voices rumbling from somewhere nearby.

Dropping to my knees, I cup his face in my hands. I suppose I'd convinced myself Pyro would see through the lies eventually, that he would be fighting any chance he got. Seething flames, raised fists ablaze. Now I realize how foolish I was, because losing Mania would debilitate me too. My fingers stretch outward to his ears, my thumbs holding his jaw. If I weren't just a spirit, I'd give him a rough shake and tell him to snap out of it. Our girl still needs us.

"Hoax?" Pyro suddenly asks, his eyes cracking to track the darkness. My body tenses, not sure if he's delirious or if he can actually sense me. A shiver rakes through his body, breaking the moment. Skidding around him on my knees, I lower myself down behind him. Wrapping my arms around Pyro's bare chest, I spoon him in the hopes he really can sense me. That in a tiny, insignificant way, I might just be bringing him some comfort. I'm sure Ghost would have a few choice words about this situation, but something tells me it's not as strange as it should probably seem.

I remain there until the rhythmic rise and fall of Pyro's chest signals he's fallen asleep. I'm thankful for that alone, knowing how long the nights can stretch on when forced to remain awake. In the time it's taken for Pyro to find his reprieve, my anger has only intensified. Burning rage licks at my being, the promise of revenge on repeat in my mind. Giving him one last squeeze, I stand tall and close my eyes again. This time, I don't picture someone I care about. I imagine a cunning smile framed by wrinkles. White hair to match the thick eyebrows hovering over a set of piercing blue eyes. And upon opening my eyes; there he is, staring straight through me.

I'm tempted to side-step just to dodge the intense, blue stare but I hold my ground. A simple t-shirt with three buttons at the neck clings to a body that should belong to someone much younger than him. This close, I also notice the reduction of wrinkles lining his face and the inch of dark hair breaking free at the roots of his white combover.

Watching himself intently in the mirror behind me, Christopher drags on a thick, woollen cardigan but not before I see the hundreds of pinprick marks lining each of his forearms. Some are clearly new, although the evidence of thin scars underneath are barely visible anymore. Reaching for his cane, Christopher gives himself an approving look before walking through the modest bedroom, dragging his cane behind him. I watch him disappear, unease prickling at my senses.

Scanning the room, from its visible en-suite bathroom and walk-in shower, to the slickness of his mahogany furniture and monotone, geometric bedspread, I absorb every detail. A canvas hangs above the bed, splashed with bold strokes that add the only color to the room. Everything screams money, yet the man I just saw leave is dressed so humbly.

With long strides, I follow to the staircase. Framed photos hang from the left wall, each one presenting a carefully positioned figure and a beaming smile. Christopher is in most of them, alongside a gray-haired woman I would presume is his wife. Other than the hordes of children appearing several times over, one image in particular grabs my attention. An old man who I thought was Christopher kneels proudly with a young boy at his side. Through the faded coloring, both wear a white lab coat, although the boys is far too large and hangs from his tiny shoulders. In the scientist's hand, a needle is primed and paused over the boy's forearm long enough for the pair to smile at the camera. With the caption 'The Day It All Began,' it's only fitting to presume I'm looking at the original Mutant scientist; and the young boy who bears a resemblance to the evil bastard that now owns an asylum of Mutes.

Laughter rings through the lower level, drawing me down the stairs and towards a sun-kissed garden. Stepping out onto the veranda, I try to imagine briefly what it would be like for the shining sun to wash over my skin, to be a part of the laughter all around. Since the day I appeared in Mania's hospital room, I've felt nothing but confusion. Billowing smoke from a BBQ floats through me, as does the jet spray of children chasing each other with water pistols. A long table of food lines the patio, and in the center, a beaming Christopher is passing out bottled drinks.

"Thanks Pap," a voice replies, accepting his offering. A frown hitches between my eyebrows, my brain seeming to comprehend what my memories can't. That voice is oddly familiar and belongs to a petite blonde with the physique of a Pitbull. A long blonde braid hangs down the back of a floral summer dress, at odds with the bulky muscles of her arms and calves. Her blue eyes flick around before she steps into her father's personal space, as do I to hear her muttered words.

"Is everything ready for our fiery friend?" she whispers. My spirit freezes, the blonde's identity coming back to me. She was in the lab when the machine holding my body was shut off. I was too distracted by watching myself die all over again, and losing Mania's companionship all at once to pay attention to faces, but I remember her now. Lorraine - Christopher's daughter and the warden of Hermitage Orphanage for Mute Boys. Curling my fingers around her throat, I will all my power into choking her in that moment, but nothing happens.

"Not here Lorraine," Christopher bites back harshly. "No business talk while your mother is home. Once the nurses return to collect her, I'll show you exactly how ready we are." A glint of satisfaction sparkles in his blue eyes, softening further as a gray-haired woman from the photos approaches. Like her daughter, her hair swishes down to her lower back and she too has dressed up for the occasion. A floaty skirt moves freely around her legs as she edges a zimmer frame closer.

"Hey Ma," Lorraine tries to help the older woman, who reels back in shock.

"Who are you? Get off me!" she cries. Christopher barges Lorraine out of the way, bending to catch his wife's attention.

"Shhh Martha, it's okay. I'm here. Come back to me, my love," he soothes calmly. The woman catches sight of his blue eyes, her rigidness eases.

"Christopher?" she frowns, causing the creases in her face to intensify. "Why do you look so old?" A collective chuckle sounds from the adults tucked beneath gazebos, a hidden joke going unspoken. Taking his wife's hands, Christopher helps her to shuffle into the center of the grass, his support meaning the zimmer frame can be left behind. Noting his cue, someone turns up the speakers with a song that makes Martha gasp in happiness.

"Our wedding song, my dear. Do you remember?" Christopher asks softly, gently pulling his wife against his firm chest.

"How could I forget? It just happened," Martha replies, falling into step with her husband. Resting her head on his shoulder, the others watch with contented smiles. The song drifts through the air as easily as the afternoon breeze, the children enjoying their water fight and the smoke billowing from the BBQ as the food is about ready to eat. It's perfect.

So completely fucking perfect, I snap my hands into fists, look to the sky and bellow with all my might. Every ounce of anger I can't expel in any other way escapes my spirit on a silent scream the living world remains oblivious to. The injustice of my brother lying on a cell floor while an expression of love and admiration is plastered all over Christopher's stupid face is too much to bear. A love Christopher Gordon doesn't deserve and I vow to steal from him.

As if called on by the very intensity of my cry, a rogue lightning bolt zaps through the cloudless sky. Spiraling downwards, its target is clear. Encased in a purple hue, it crackles with the intensity of hatred I feel in the pit of my soul. Hurtling towards Christopher's head, the lightning bolt splits into four just before it destroys him. Instead, each new spoke blasts in the directions of the speakers, exploding them with an almighty display of sparks. My chest heaves, my eyes ablaze in my head as if I were actually real. The world comes distorted, filtering the masses of people running for the safety of the house in a film of purple. All except Christopher and Lorraine.

"Get your mother to safety," Christopher barks at a tall man who has taken the old woman beneath his arm. Nodding similar blue eyes at his father, the man ushers the rest of the children inside and locks the patio door firmly behind them.

"What do you think it was?" Lorraine asks, both her and Christopher staring at the sun-soaked sky.

"Not a natural phenomenon," Christopher growls darkly. "Call for the MRA. They can deal with this. Today is my anniversary and I promised myself an official day off." Lorraine has a phone pulled from her pocket and glued to her ear as the pair head towards the house, plastering wide smiles for the spectators pressed against the windows.

"Day off?" I ask no one in particular. "Where's Pyro's fucking day off?!" Darting for the closest telephone pole, I rest my hands on where the wood should smooth against my palms. Although I hate to agree with that evil bastard, that lightning bolt wasn't a coincidence - it was me. And just like I managed to break the statue at the graveyard, I know I can shatter Christopher's façade of a peaceful day. Closing my eyes, I focus my energy. Release my mind of any thoughts that aren't dark, any feelings that aren't bitter. Especially those of Mania which fill me with guilt and longing. What I need right now is the overriding resentment I hope isn't part of who I really am.

A few sparks splutter from my palms and die out, my teeth gritted in concentration. Tuning into a low chuckle, I crack an eye to see Christopher is at the doorway now, his arm around Lorraine and his lying lips telling everyone the party will continue inside. Suddenly, a surge of power flows through me and into the pole. Shoving all of my being into that feeling, the electric volt flies upwards, colliding with the wires. Sparks rain down, accompanied by the groan of the entire street's electric short-circuiting out. A satisfied smile takes residence on my face until I try to pull back.

By some force I don't understand, my hands are stuck. The power flows through me freely until I try to pull away. The swirling purple energy darkens to black and instead of being expelled, it turns on me. Shooting back into my spirit, I cry out at the assault I shouldn't be able to feel. Piercing, slicing and gutting me from the inside. Breaking free of my body, a cloud of darkened fog surrounds me. And right before my eyes, the smoke twists into blackened spears that shoot into my chest. Holy fucking ow. Tugging at my hands, I remain stuck to the pole, screaming through the whooshing passing through my ears.

Pinned in place by the spears, I can merely watch through tear-filled eyes as flakes of my tattooed skin begin to separate from my arms. The inked wires that seemed integrated into my being dissipate and swirl around the cloud closing in on me. No. I'm fading. I'm disappearing, and all because of some petty desire to ruin Christopher's joy.

"Hoaxxxx," a voice hisses through the black smoke. "I. Fucking. Warned. You." A hand snaps closed around my wrist, the first physical contact I've felt since Mania and I were last in Hell together. Yanking me free from the telephone pole, I come nose-level with a face altered by the Devil himself. Lava bubbles beneath the skin, disappearing under Asher's specs, although his burning eyes are closed. His brows tense in concentration. A grunt escapes my lips, the spears of dark smoke flying outward from my spirit. Released from their hold, I too push against the smoke, condensing it into a churning ball of hatred that plows into Asher's chest.

As quickly as it started, I'm thrown back from the pole and tossed across the grass beneath the sun's glare. Not a trace of darkness can be seen as I twist and choke out the last of the agony that so recently claimed me.

"You can't stay here," Asher grits out, rising to his feet and patting himself down. Whether he's accustomed to the pain of the fog or simply squashed it, there's no evidence Asher is feeling the effects like I did.

"Whatever happened to settling unfinished business?" I drawl, sitting up with my knees to my chest. I'm not sure if I can stand currently, and don't want to give Asher any more evidence that I'm not in control. Crossing the distance between us, he lowers onto his haunches and sighs.

"Staying will only ensure you never see Mania again. You can't help her, but at least in Hell, you can wait for her." For the first time, as he peers over his spec, I see a softness in Asher's burnt eyes. A knowledge that losing someone for eternity isn't worth the risk, whether it be a loved one or ourselves. Yet I can't agree. Helping

Mania on her suicide mission to save my body is my last hope. Even if this power destroys my soul, it will be worth it to hold her. To kiss her, to love her with whatever spirit I have left. Thankfully with a huff of understanding, Asher plants his fist on the ground and disappears before I need to explain that to him.

T he blaring of a train horn snaps my eyes open, my surroundings nothing like I was expecting when I sent out a call to find Mania. A busy train station buzzes with life all around, between coffee shops and bustling platforms. Looking either side, it's my ears that pick up on Mania's sweet voice first.

"-blending in. I thought that was the point of this," she strides towards a bench, flicking her purple hair. I realize now why I didn't recognize her at first. Both Mania and Ghost have altered their appearances to blend in like any other human couple. A short summer dress and light jacket do little to disguise the shiver in Mania's limbs, but the purple hair and makeup concealing the crack in her forehead mask her well. Aside from the black shoe polish in his hair, Ghost even goes as far as to draw Mania beneath his arm once she's re-joined the bench.

Lifting his hand, Ghost waves cheerily in my direction and I balk, quickly twisting to look behind me. A male in a polo shirt and dark jeans stands on the opposite platform, dragging his limbs towards a pedestrian bridge that connects the two. I narrow my eyes, watching him the entire way until he perches on the far end of the bench, his elbows on his thighs. Ghost seems comfortable in the male's presence but I don't miss the frequent side glances Mania can't hide. She doesn't trust him, which means I'll be keeping him in my sights from here on out.

"How cozy," another male comments dryly. This one strolled out of nowhere, his oversized jersey and muddy sneakers out of place with the group. Apparently a lot has happened in my time at Christopher's. Knocking Ghost's foot aside with his shoe, my brother withdraws his arm from Mania's shoulders to stand.

"You were meant to ditch the car, not fuck it," Ghost smirks and I bristle. Either Ghost finds it incredibly easy to make new friends, or he's the master of masking his feelings. The newest male scrubs at a grease mark on his cheek, taking Ghost's lead to walk straight through me. I stand still, letting them all go until Mania moves to follow. With all my might, I wish I could materialize just in time for her to bump into my chest, my hands able to wipe away the worry lines causing her makeup to crease. But it's useless. So I turn and follow the group all the way to the furthest platform. Posturing themselves against the wall, the four not-so-secretively wait for the camera overhead to find a new target.

"Now what?" Mania asks, her teeth chattering. Hugging her arms around herself, I step into her side, for whatever good it's worth.

"Now we wait," Ghost growls back. Wait for what, I couldn't say. Only that all traces of the jokey, easy-going male I just saw has disappeared without a trace. Instead, a meticulous leader rests against the wall, his eyes absorbing every detail of the station around him. From the open sunlight overhead, to the shining rails lining the tracks. Before long, the speakers crackle with the incoming of an announcement.

'Attention all passengers, the next scheduled train on platform two is not scheduled to stop at this station. Please stand back and remain behind the yellow lines until the train has passed. Thank you.'

The rhythmic beat of the train rolling down the tracks increases until a roar is upon us, the impending flash of chrome imminent. Rolling my head to the side, my mind wanders to a different time. A different world, where all Mutes are accepted and a day trip out with friends was a common occurrence. These trains could take us anywhere we wanted to go if only-

A short scream escapes Mania and I jolt upright, my hands fisted and ready. The train across the tracks is flying through the station at an incredible speed, just like the announcement said it would, with no other dangers in sight. That is until I see the mangled remains of what appears to be a woman crushed beneath the wheels, her head of black hair bobbing with each new carriage. In a flash, the train has disappeared from view, and so has Mania. Ghost whips out from the door he was waiting by to grab the two males still standing in shock and drags them inside. I'm about to follow too, when someone else catches my eye.

Screams ring out at the woman's distorted body lying in the ditch below. Children are crying and men are shouting for a doctor, although it seems a little late for that. At odds with the surroundings, a pair of horns stand out among the crowds both disgusted and stepping closer to get a better look. Tanned skin and green eyes I recognize drop from the platform's edge and land on the rails with her knees bent. To top it off, a glowing scepter is clutched in her hand.

"Azella," I breathe to myself. As if she heard me, her head snaps upwards, her eyes locking on mine. Fuck, it feels so good to be *seen*. Shifting through space easily this time, I'm standing in front of Azella as quickly as it takes to blink.

"Hoax," she mimics back, standing to stare at me curiously. "I haven't seen you or Mania around in a while. It's not like her to behave enough to stay alive for so long," she offers me a half smile around one fang. Although, one look at the graveness on my face and all trace of mirth leaves her. "What's happened?"

"It's a long story, but you're here now. I need your help." I nod matter-of-factly. For the first time since I became completely invisible, a glimmer of hope wells inside.

"Hoax, I can't stay. I'm...working," Azella looks at the body by her feet. Even she winces at the state of the corpse, and that's from a demon of Hell. The woman's bones are utterly shattered, piercing the trampled layer of skin that remains almost everywhere. "I can only stay on Earth as long as I've been tasked with a soul to reap. But I can meet you later, outside the gates. I'll do my best to help you then." It's my turn to grimace at the thought of returning to Hell just to find myself dragged through the fires of no return.

"I can't risk making it easier for Asher," I grunt. "Seems I'm his particular soul to reap at current." Azella's eyebrows raise in surprise and I huff. "I knew it, the summons was bogus."

"Oh no, you misread me. If Asher is relieved of guard duty, the summons must be real. I may be the Devil's right-hand demon but I'm not privy to all communications he sends. I'm assuming Asher has been given a chance to work off the rest of his sentence and you're his payment." Growling beneath my breath, I kick out my canvas shoe, surprised when the dead woman's foot knocks aside on impact.

"I refuse to leave," I grit out. Azella's eyes are trained on the shifted foot too, her eyes filled with curiosity.

"I see," she nods with a sigh. Humans have gathered on the platform above. Some taking pictures on their phones, others screaming at the horrible sight but find themselves unable to look away.

"Fine. Meet me at Rosefield cemetery. Demons are able to pass through burial grounds undetected for short spaces of time. I'll sneak away at some point tonight. You'll just have to wait until I'm able to get there." Stamping her scepter on the track, Azella kneels to place a hand on her victim. Gold swirls from the staff's point of contact with the ground, seeming to draw on the Earth itself for power. Although the body remains broken and mushed like a trodden-on strawberry, a perfectly formed version of the dark-haired woman peels out of her corpse and floats directly into Azella's chest. Shuddering, she gives me the briefest of nods before disappearing completely.

A pair of medics run down the platform in fluorescent yellow, a stretcher in their hands. Dropping down from the ledge, unknowingly beside me, they begin to scoop up what's left of the woman when another group catches my eye. Blue shirts, purposeful strides towards the maintenance door. Afterlife lanyards swaying from their necks. Shit - Mania!

Launching myself after the guards, the space between us disappears as I find myself at the back of the last guard. This teleporting thing is definitely going to come in handy. The four pass through the maintenance doorway, paying no mind to the camera that tracks their movements overhead. I stay close, spotting a darkened staircase ahead. Phasing my spirit to the front, I navigate the curved stairwell in short bursts of how far ahead I can see. The bottom levels out in a series of forgotten underground tunnels, each hosting a decayed excuse for tracks. The darkness is broken up by lanterns every so often, causing the shadows to thrive but there's no sign of the Mutes that disappeared down here.

Hopping on impatient feet, the guards finally stroll to ground level and lazily head in the direction of the tunnel directly in front. Perfect, a direction. With a mix of space-hopping and running, I vow to get there in plenty of time to…well I don't know what I can do but the past few days have proven I'm not as useless as I believed. The tunnel is miles long easily, and after a while I stop with a frown. There's no way those guards, walking at their relaxed pace, will travel this far on foot. Instead, I backtrack until I meet up with the four of them as they come to a halt. The one I'd class as the leader, a muscled man with a goatee, pulls out a key fob and presses it against a minuscule touch pad on the wall. I'd completely missed it, and they probably would too if not for the shadow of an indent against the cold rockface.

"Took you long enough," a graveled voice says as the rock moves aside to reveal a concealed room. "What, did you stop for a lunch date on the way?" The man speaking from inside takes a shirt from a hook on the wall, and shrugs it onto his bare shoulders. Something seems odd about the skeletal ridges of his torso and the tallied tattoos slipping in and out of his exposed ribs. Not what I'd expect of an Afterlife guard. He buttons up the shirt regardless, pulling a pair of polished shoes out of an oblong chest and swapping them from his heavy steel-capped-toed boots. There's nothing else in there except a cart on wheels and a trash chute in the ceiling above it.

"There was a disturbance at the boss' house. We could have used your talents over there instead-"

"Instead of letting you guys fuck up the packing like last time?" he cuts off the leader, clicking his fingers at the crate. "Let's get this job done. My girl is waiting for me." That's when I decide this guy isn't a guard. I can't pinpoint why exactly, call it a gut feeling. It could be to do with his blue-tipped hair or the deadened haze to his bottomless eyes, or maybe it's more than that. The guards find too much enjoyment in their position, beating on Mutes and locking them up. Not begrudging their job like this male clearly does.

The lackeys who have yet to speak move forward to tug out the crate, putting all their effort into dragging it onto the train tracks. A gap has been strategically cut from the metal for the wheels to merge onto the tracks. From there, it only takes one of them to shove the container forward, one of the broken wheels causing a nasty screech every time it rolls over. Stepping out with the two that remain by the cart, the male stops to receive the key fob from the leader. He tilts his head, looking around the tunnel before setting in my direction. A trace of gold slithers through his otherwise dull irises', sending the leader into full alert.

"You sense something?"

"Maybe. I'm not sure," he frowns, confused by his own words. Shrugging, he takes a side of the cart and the three of them begin to tug it forward, leaving two others back in the room with the open chute. Trepidation crawls up my spine and like before, I jump ahead through the tunnels en route with the tracks. It doesn't take long before I come across someone. A grumbling male with shoe polish coating his usual milk-white hair. Ghost, and he's walking directly towards the oncoming cart and guards. Panic flares to life as my head whips back and forth. He needs to move, hide, run, something.

Passing through my body on dragged feet, I slam my hand down on Ghost's arm, shouting in his ear for him to stop. A hiss escapes his lips, his eyes flying to the handprint sizzling through his sleeve into his skin. I halt, staring at the slithers of purple swirling around my fingers as I continue to burn a mark into my brother. He hunts for me frantically until the wheels of the cart grind closer. Shoving himself through the closest wall, I sigh in relief at his narrow escape.

Lifting my hand up to inspect my glowing hand, the male pretending to be a guard narrows his eyes in my direction again. I draw the power back into me, concealing me from whatever 'talents' the leader spoke of. The crate hits a bump in the tracks then, and an arm flops out from beneath the covers. Tossing it back inside, the male secures the cover in place and continues on his way. I keep my distance from him, moving through the tunnel ahead at lightning speed until I find who I'm looking for.

Even in her disguised state, the sight of Mania fills me with equal amounts of flutters and dread. She's having a heart-to-heart with the male beside her, speaking as if they're old friends but there's no time for that now. Like before, I call out, shout her name and try to touch her. Nothing works. My hand passes through her body as the squeak of the wheel echoes around the tunnel, causing the pair to spin. To his credit, the male puts himself in front of Mania for protection until she pulls the pair of them into a hidden crevice in the wall. I hope it would be enough, but from my advantage point, the brightness of the male's jersey does nothing to conceal them both.

The male walking alongside the crate spots them instantly, his feet halting. "Something wrong, Detective?" a guard asks, deepening my understanding of what's happening here. He's a Mute that can sense others. Perfect. Growing rigid, his body stiffens at the same time his eyes begin to change. From bland to pure gold, I watch them intensify until his eyeballs are like burning coals in his skull. Whatever he's doing has an effect on the male hiding Mania too, allowing him to be chucked aside by the closest guard.

"Mania! Run!" I yell at the top of my lungs. Whether she hears me or by coincidence, she does just that. But she's not quick enough. The guard pushing the crate whips after her, caging an arm around her fragile human body. Lifting her off her feet, Mania fights the best she can but she's no match. Tossing her onto the covered crate, he delivers a blow to her temple, halting her efforts to get away. And the entire time, I keep snapping my hands into fists, calling on the mysterious power which evades me now. Come on, where the fuck is it?! Roaring at the ceiling, I feel a tremor of the electricity that consumed me before. Images assault my mind of the smoke turning on me, spearing me with a strength I couldn't control, but I shove the thoughts away. I need the power now, no matter of the repercussions. I need to save my girl.

The guard pins Mania down by her throat, and dammit all to hell, she doesn't even fight. Tension leaves her limbs, her eyes half open and it occurs to me then. She's given up. My tie to her is weak because she feels she is. If only I can show her the strength we could create together. Stepping through the guard, I peer down at my mate, willing her to see me.

"Mania, I need you to fight or we won't stand a chance. Come on sweetheart. You're better than this." Drawing my lips over where hers lay parted, I will those words to seep into her soul like a mantra. We can do this. We've come too far to quit now. Rolling her head aside, Mania spies Ghost fighting with everything he has to get to her. His battle cries project from behind a film of blood, most of which I'm sure isn't his. The 'Detective' is flattened on the ground and the other guard has resorted to using a baton. "That's it Mania. Feel how much we want you, how many people we'd kill for you."

A gasp escapes her lips at the same moment I feel it. A surge of heat, energy and something uniquely Mania. A toxic combination of grit and death she wraps herself in to survive. I allow it to fill me, consume me. Scrunching her eyes tight and digging her nails into the arm holding her down, I exhume every trickle of power I process in this fleeting moment and push it into her body. A blinding light bursts between us, sending her captive flying across the tunnel. And still, I focus on gifting her the entirety of my devotion. I may not remember my life pre-Mania, but I know somehow, in some way, she was meant for me.

As the light between us dies to barely a shimmer, a strong pair of tattooed arms thrust through me to lift Mania from the crate. She's crushed into Ghost's chest, his breath sawing in and out audibly. Not from exertion but from fear. Briefly closing his eyes and resting his cheek on her head, I stand in the center, pretending to do the same. Drinking in the moment of the three of us together, I almost miss the words Ghost whispers into Mania's ear.

"I need you to run." Without giving her a choice, he dumps Mania onto unsteady feet and nudges her away as a wave of dizziness washes through me. I falter, confused by the feeling my spirit shouldn't be able to feel. Yet with the loss of Mania's presence, my being blinks in and out of sight, my hands fading as if my very life force is being sucked away with her.

Stumbling aside, I bend over, supporting myself on my knees. I can't throw up but my eyes are swimming, unable to focus on one spot as I say the same phrase over and over in my mind. Rosefield Cemetery. I need to meet Azella. I need to shift my spirit at least one more time if I have any hopes of help. Of continuing my time on Earth. In slow motion, the tunnel around me tilts. My head sways and my body follows. Toppling onto the ground, I register the sea of grass and towering headstones just before my world turns black.

"Wakey, wakey," a voice says, a click sounds by my ear. I stir, rolling onto my front and pushing myself up to my knees. If I remembered what a hangover felt like, this would be a killer one. The graveyard is pitch black, shrouded by the clouded night blocking out any sight of the moon. It takes me a moment to sift through my recent memories that brought me to this moment and place. One thought slams into my skull with a sudden rise of panic. Mania and Ghost. Are they safe? Did they escape the tunnels?

"They're no longer in the tunnels if that answers your question," the voice comes again and I now realize I spoke out loud. "But they're not safe either. All the more reason to work on controlling the power you can't handle." Scowling up, the man looming over me isn't the demon I intended to meet.

"Finally decided to help me then," I growl at Asher, pushing myself to my feet. The lava coursing through the side of his face is quelled, trickling slowly through the exposed scars. Having ditched the glasses, his golden eyes regard me with indignation as he stretches out a hand to help me up. I ignore it, pushing myself up to his height. "What happened to not resisting the summons?"

"Azella." Asher shrugs, dropping his hand. Leaning back on a headstone, I spot the specter by his feet along with a thick set of metal cuffs. "She tried to pull rank on me, but I saw it for what it was. Desperation. That little twit you all love has a hold I don't understand, but I have a job to do."

"Call Mania that again and we'll see exactly what this power of mine can do," I threaten. My eyes keep reverting back to those cuffs, challenging Asher to try and get me in them. I may be unstable, but I know I'm powerful. As long as it answers when I call, I'll put Asher on his ass again without a moment's hesitation.

"Relax. I bear Mania no ill will. She's been a thorn in my side since she started appearing in Hell at eight years old. Running back and forth through the fires, riling up the prisoners, playing hide and seek with my specter. And that was just a few months ago," he smiles dryly to himself. My hackles ease and suddenly I see Asher in a new light. Azella may have been the one to adopt Mania as her own, but there are more demons that took on the family roles in her life. Just like Asher, who has unknowingly become the bored older brother who secretly cares.

"So...you've come up here to teach me how to control my power, which I will inevitably use to evade your summons. Seems counterproductive from your perspective." I fold my arms as Asher's half smirk.

"There's always a catch, Hoax. I've made an agreement with Azella to train you. But only if, once Mania is seen safe from her current predicament, you hand yourself over to me. Your spirit doesn't belong up here. There might not even be anything left to reap and I'll be on gate duty for an eternity, but Mania can take my spot when her time is finally up. As long as it's when she's old and decrepit."

"You care for her," I say without a trace of judgment. The simple truth Asher neither confirms nor denies, but it's so obvious now, I don't know how I missed it before. He's perfected his nonchalant attitude, that's for sure. Nodding my head, I hold my hand out. "I will hand my spirit over when Mania is safe and free."

"She'll never be free. Whether she's officially a Mute or not, she's of interest to those seeking for answers. Like the rest of your gang, she'll be constantly hunted until she runs out of places to hide."

"Very well," I agree. "How about this - I will see Mania freed from Christopher's clutches. Then I'm all yours." Asher steps forward, grasping my hand and sealing our deal with a golden glow that matches his brightening eyes. Content that I don't need to worry about him dragging me to the underworld as soon as my back is turned, a new air filters around Asher and I. Lifting his scepter, he gestures for me to take a hold. The instant my fingers graze the wood, we're shifted into a setting polar opposite to where we were.

The brightness of the sun burns my eyes and I don't need to be physically present to sense the stifling heat beaming down on us. Sand rolls for as far as the eye can see, dipping and rising in dunes of yellow ripples. Nothing and no one else can survive out here, making it the perfect place to learn to control my power.

"Where are we?" I ask, patting myself down to check all of me made the journey.

"The short answer would be the Sahara Desert," Asher rolls his neck, releasing a few cracks in doing so. Catching my eye, he tuts, moving on to circle his shoulders. "The long answer is the Sahara, on a different astral plane. The specters can transport us through dimensions as well as space. If you're not careful, you could stumble across an alternate version of yourself. One with a backbone, perhaps." I snap my head his way when the horizon caught my gaze, and although I'm fairly sure that was his attempt at a joke, I huff through my nostrils.

"Where do we start then?" I ask impatiently, straightening said backbone. The longer I spend out here trying to get a handle on myself, the longer Mania could be in trouble and needing my help. The worst thing would be to sharpen my spiritual tools, only to be too late to use them. Asher thrusts the specter into the sand, abandoning it upright to take my hands in his. He stares at my palms before laying his flat on top, closing his eyes. I stand there, waiting for something to happen. It doesn't.

"Well?" Asher's eyes open to narrow at me and he drops my hands.

"I don't have all the answers. Aside from the imbalance of your soul wandering around while your body is technically alive, the energy connected to your spirit is a mixture of Pyro's eternal flame and the connection to your physical body. I'm guessing those pinpricks in your arm were there when you were alive?" I look down, spotting the tiny scars disappearing into my tattoos that I've never seen before. Rolling my arms over, Asher grunts. "Seems like they've been testing your body and injecting you with fuck knows what. We have no idea what we're contending with here. It's a fucking mess in all honesty, but we'll give it a try."

"Real comforting, thanks," I drawl sarcastically. Cracking my head side to side because it felt like the right thing to do, I roll my shoulders and raise my hands. I just need to focus on a strong emotion like last time and something should answer my call. Anger. Anger is easiest.

Flooding my mind with images of those I love being tortured by those I despise, a simmer of electricity passes through my chest and floats down my arms, but nothing external is produced. I frown, focusing harder. Going a step further, I imagine Pyro on the cell floor, bloodied and unbreathing to fuel the flames he supposedly gifted me. A soft purple hue glows at the end of my fingertips, but again, nothing of use.

"Fuck," I growl, dropping my hands. "This is stupid. It came so much easier when I was angry before."

"Try this," Asher strolls forward. Wrapping his hand around my wrist, he pulls my hand down to the sand. Urging my fingers into the sand, the lava beneath his skin begins to pulse. A force is pushed into my wrist where Asher is holding me still, his own power seeping through my hand. Inky black patterns swirl through the sand and I shift at the weight of it. Not physically, but Asher's energy is clearly that of a demon. A remaining echo of perished souls coiling around my being until the taste of burnt tar crawls up the back of my throat. I try to cough it out, shuddering at the feeling of deceased screams intoxicating my bloodstream.

"Focus," he grunts, jerking his head at the sand. "Use my power to create a tornado in the sand. Start small." Pressing my lips together, I do as he says. All of my concentration centers on the black patterns, willing them to form one continuous circle. When I've achieved this, I curl my hand to draw the swirling energy higher, forming a mini whirlpool of sand beneath it. "Good. Now expand it slowly. Keep it in your control at all times. We want the tornado to surround us without dragging our beings into a thousand tiny particles that can't be put back together."

I grit my teeth, ignoring Asher's lack of pep talk skills. Keeping my sights directly on the small storm within my hand, I spread my fingers, encouraging the sandstorm to grow. Asher's hand remains on my wrist, preparing to step in if need be but this is all me. The particles spread wider, picking up more sand and speed. Passing around us, the tornado grows until we're sitting in the eye of the storm, watching it stretch towards the sky. I smile, feeling utterly accomplished when a pained hiss leaves Asher's lips.

"Something's...wrong," he shudders. I try to yank my wrist away from his bone-crushing hold, clenching my fist closed and realizing too late that was a terrible idea. The storm slams closed over us but doesn't stop spinning. Instead, we're trapped inside with the weight of the sand thundering down on us. In this realm, it doesn't seem to matter that I'm a spirit. As the particles turn blackened like ash, they slice at my skin. Millions of tiny slashes and splinters finding my face as I duck into my arms, panicked more by Asher's cries than whatever scrapes of skin I have left.

"Stop!" I yell out, suddenly standing and throwing my arms out wide. A bolt of purple lighting pierces the tornado, slamming directly into my chest and tossing me aside. The sand drops lifelessly from the sky and by the time I've rolled onto my side, all that remains is a mound of sand where Asher last was. Fuck. Dragging myself forward on my cut forearms, I dig through the endless reams of sand. Every handful I scoop out, more falls instead to refill it, but soon enough I manage to start winning. Pushing my arms into the mound up to my shoulder, I feel out the roughness of Asher's leather tunic and drag him up to the surface.

"Let's...not do that again," he splutters. Gulping in lungfuls of air, Asher wriggles himself free while I tug him the rest of the way.

"We don't have a choice," I drop onto my back, exhausted and pissed beyond belief. Killed but not really dead; given a power that threatens to destroy me - seems that I can't catch a break. "I need to master it."

"Then you'd better get used to getting hurt. There's a block hindering your ability to maintain any power you temporarily possess." I twist my hand, smacking a hand down on Asher's chest when it looks like he's drifting off to sleep.

"How do I remove this block?"

"Only you can work that one out," he bats my arm away and rests his head back. "I'm just worried you're being hindered by the very thing you're trying to save."

"I'm not giving up on Mania."

"I wasn't referring to her." Twisting onto his side, Asher blinks his glazed, golden eyes my way, a small crinkle between his eyebrows. "I saw flashes of your thoughts when your mind drifted. You want to be alive again, albeit to have a life alongside her, but I'm worried your connection to your body is going to be your downfall. Whatever they're doing to you in that institute, you might not have anything to go back to." I hate the pity in Asher's expression, not to mention the intrusion of my thoughts. Of course that's what I'd prefer but I'm a realist. There's no winning this war for me, but if I can assist Mania even slightly, that'll have to be enough.

"All the reason to hurry up and work this shit out. Again," I bark, grabbing Asher's wrist and refusing to take no for an answer.

I force Asher to assist me until I know, if I hadn't been practically dead already, my body would have been ready to give up. As it stands, I can still barely maintain a purple ball of energy in my hand. I'm not sure why that's my color, but I leave it down to the hue of my hair and irises. Unlike the few times I've managed to access it in the heat of the moment, my power evades me as if it didn't call for a bolt of lightning out of a cloudless sky, twice.

"We need to get back," Asher mutters from his hunched over position. I've used his power so many times, the bitterness of blackened tar no longer feels odd. In fact, I've come to accept it. I'm Hell-bound once I'm done helping Mania anyway, might as well adjust now. Walking over, I ease Asher upright and hand him the scepter. The glass orb glows at my touch, probably from any lingering demon power I have left swirling through my veins. I open my mouth to say…well anything but I can't settle on what. Asher and I made a deal for him to train me, one that he'll benefit from ultimately so any praise or apologies die on my tongue.

Gripping the specter, Asher stamps it in the ground and in the next instant, we appear in an empty stone arena. Vines claw at any break in the stone they can find, desperate to escape the prison they're hidden beneath. Every few meters, a rounded archway stands tall. The curved walls are cragged on top, as if there once was a domed roof that's been torn down. Overhead, the early rays of sunshine bleeding into an orange sky chase away the lingering shadows of an extremely long night.

"Where-" I begin to ask when movement draws my attention to the archways. Bodies rush into the clearing from all directions, desperate for their first glimpse. Eyes of all colors dart around and I still, realizing they're all Mutes. Hundreds of them, piling into the arena and quickly running out of room to move. Yet still, they scramble over each other, trying to get a closer look at the walls. Using my transparency to walk through the crowds, I watch intently as Mutes match small numbered labels on their clothes to markings etched into each individual stone on the walls. Upon finding the corresponding number, they pop open a chamber to reveal a range of odd items lying inside.

In the distance, over the mix of elated cheers and disappointed groans at their finds, the rhythmic music of a beatboxer grows. I locate the Mute in question, surprised he has no amplifier in sight. His volume booms around the topless cavern, providing a heavy bass as a sea of drones descend overhead and a gunshot pierces the air. I spin, hunting for the source but instead, a head of black and red hair catches my attention. My feet are moving of their own accord until Asher's hand grips the back of my neck and uses his power to cement my feet in place.

Struggling to keep sight of Mania between the Mutes fleeing for safety, the next time her widened blood-red eyes appear, a pair of thickly corded arms banded around her. Ghost holds Mania's head to his chest, drawing her a few steps backwards until they disappear through a wall. I push out a sigh of relief, which quickly turns into a scowl.

"Don't keep me from helping Mania again. That was the whole point of this," I twist with my hand raised to reveal a tiny purple ball swirling in the center. Finding my feet free again, I turn fully, finding Asher isn't anywhere to be seen. What I can see though, is a shitload of spirits rising from their bodies and running around screaming. The noise is twice as loud as when they were alive, and as a woman with flowing yellow hair runs in my direction, her body collides with mine. Too stunned that she can touch me, I lose balance and hit the floor in a mess of tangled limbs.

"Get the fuck," I growl trying to shove her aside, "off of me." Hovering over my face, her neon yellow eyes begin to darken into coals of black, her jaw stretching and becoming dislocated. It's like a horror movie happening before my eyes. Her limbs crack and she falls further forward, crumpling over my body until I shove her aside.

"Hoax!" Asher shouts, appearing over me. "Take this." He throws me a second specter, this one identical to the one still clasped in his right hand. "Tap it on the ground and absorb her soul. We need all hands on deck here!" Peering over the heap of dead bodies and spirits running riot, more demons appear across the arena, catching whoever they can. The woman at my side has taken to army crawling away, despite the cracking of her limbs in awkward directions with each movement.

"Now Hoax! Before she's absorbed into the Earth!" Without sparing another thought, I push myself up onto my knees and throw the end of the specter down onto the ground. Power pulses through me, igniting the circuit tattoos along my arm and bringing the orb on top to life.

Pressing a hand over the spirit, the woman howls an ear-piercing shriek as she's absorbed into my body. Sucked straight in like vacuum. I wriggle uncomfortably at the feeling of her bashing around inside my being but I don't have time to adjust. A second later, I'm exactly where I didn't want to be. Staring at the iron gates of Hell with the fires blazing all the way up to the clouded, lightless sky. Even from the end of the chained prisoner line, I can feel the heat and I take a tentative step back.

"A newbie, huh?" I look across to a demon lifting the shackle from the charred grass. Aside from his stout, muscled body, he bears no resemblance to any other demons I've seen up to this point. His vibrant green eyes peer out from the face of a hog. Long tusks curl upwards from his bottom row of teeth, framing the pig-like snout that has a meaty piercing hanging between his nostrils. Pointed ears poke out of his straggly hair and the fingers gripping his staff are short and stubbled.

Briefly closing his eyes, a spirit is pulled out of his chest and placed directly in line with the others, hands already cuffed and his fate sealed. Behind him, another shackle appears on the ground and the demon gestures for me to pick it up. "Better be quick, we've got many more about to come in and you'll find yourself waiting for hell knows how long."

With the woman still rattling around inside like a cannon bowl in a wooden hut and her shriek piercing my inner eardrums, I grab the shackles and copy what the demon did. Eyes closed, focusing on the sheer will to get this bitch out of my body. I dislodge her and on an exhale, nudge her out of my spirit and into the cuffs. Another pair appear behind her in time for the next demon and Hog-Face smirks at me.

"Come on then, let's get back to it. Don't want to miss all the action." He vanishes and my eyes slide to the specter clutched in my hand. Okay, I guess I'm doing this. Tapping it on the ground with my destination in mind, I reappear in the arena.

Everywhere I look, demons are grabbing rogue spirits trying to flee. Nothing connects the Devil's reapers, except for the tattoo of an eye I spot imprinted on them all in visible areas. More than a few deliver their chosen target a beating before reaping their souls, which seems rather redundant after they're already dead but who am I to judge. Asher is currently battling with a huge guy, double his size with a bullet hole in the center of his forehead. Even in spirit, his skin is cracked with a reddish hue and I imagine his name was 'Brick' or similar.

"Little help here?" Asher shouts, launching himself on the spirit's back. Unsure what to do, I use the specter in my hand as a bat and swipe it through the air. The orb connects with Brick's mouth, sending a few teeth flying that disappear upon leaving his mouth. Catching him off guard, Asher wrestles his arm around the spirit's neck and wrestles him down sideways. Tapping his own staff on the ground, Brick roars as he's drawn into Asher's chest. The demon's scarred face contorts and winces before he too evaporates and leaves me hunting for my next victim.

"Over here, my man," Hog-Face calls out. His stubbled hands are wrapped around a set of conjoined twins, joined from hip to shoulder. To make up for the loss of an arm on their attached side, both women have an extra two arms and legs, giving them the appearance of a crazed octopus. I can't imagine what their use was when alive but since they're dead now, I run over and take the arm of the one who isn't punching wildly in all directions. Mine seems to understand there's no use in fighting.

Hog-Face stamps down his staff and draws the Mute closest into his chest with a banshee's scream. Ripping their joined body clean in half, she disappears and leaves my twin staring at the ribs and organs now exposed along her side. This is not a day I'll be forgetting anytime soon. Following Hog-Face's lead, I'm soon in Hell once more, waiting my turn behind masses of demons to shackle the forlorn girl behind her sister.

"Quite the natural, ain't ya?" Hog-Face smirks around his tusks. Patting me on the back, he snorts to himself. "Usually takes new recruits a while to get used to traveling by specter. You just got straight on with it, but I suppose Asher's private lesson has helped." He disappears before I can ask what he meant by that and when I shift back to the arena, Hog-Face is nowhere to be seen. The space between the stone walls is clear now, other than a single living Mute who is dragging the bodies into a neat pile. I watch him heave one on top of the next and press his hands to the base where the bodies begin to incinerate until a shout catches my attention.

"Hoax!" Running through the archway in the general direction of the sound, I keep coming to dead ends until remembering I don't need to abide by any floorplan of the maze we've found ourselves in. I shout back, returning Asher's call as I stride through wall after wall, becoming more lost. "This way!" he calls back but it's no use. I'll never find him like this.

Noting the staff still clutched in my hand, I knock it against the vine-infested floor, picturing Asher's face in my mind. He grunts, springing my eyes open as he rushes past, his shoulder slamming into mine. I curse him out, taking chase, even though I don't know what for or what from.

"Wanna fill me in?" I ask, catching up to his side. Asher has plenty of muscle on my lean frame, but in this instance, my litheness works in my favor. I could outrun him with a twisted ankle if I felt like it. The veins trailing his arms are heated with the lava coursing through his body and the smoke billowing from his beard is thick.

"One got away," Asher grunts. My head snaps up in time to see the outline of a figure shoot around the next corner.

"And...? Can't we just catch up to him later? I need to make sure Mania-"

"She's fine. She's got Ghost." Asher barks harshly. "If this shithead escapes, we're all screwed anyway. This is the best way to help right now." I frown, not realizing a demon would pursue their bounty so relentlessly. In all honesty, I hadn't thought about it before but figured spirits found their own ways to the underworld.

"Surely it's just one guy," I roll my eyes, keeping up my pace with lengthy strides.

"Haven't you been listening?" Asher grumbles, reaching up to slap the back of my head. "An un-reaped soul causes an imbalance and who knows what that could trigger. Weaker souls disintegrate into the Earth if left unchecked, poisoning the soil. Crops die, animals eating the grass become diseased. Before you know it, we'll have a plague on our hands." Rushing into another clearing, this one smaller with only a tall cage situated in the middle, we start to gain on the spirit Asher seems to begrudge.

"But a strong one like this, who can break my specter and make a run for it, he's trouble. And guess who he is fucking assigned to?" Asher drawls sarcastically. Ignoring the oblivious being that resembles a Minotaur in the cage, we sprint towards the archway the spirit disappeared through. Although instead of following, I run directly through the wall to the left in an attempt to cut in front of him. Somehow he's already at the other end of the alley, his mocking laugh trailing behind.

"Exactly why hasn't this guy turned into a broken zombie like the others?"

"Must have something to do with his ability," Asher mutters. Rushing onwards, we round a corner as he skids to a swift halt. I whip out the staff in my hand, stopping him from toppling over the edge of an opening in the ground. Filled with spikes that would be silver if it weren't for the chunks of flesh and blood coating every spoke, the spirit on the far end skids to a halt. His cocky smile is mirrored by a strangely straight moustache and goatie, and the metal ring in his eyebrow jolts as he chuckles and salutes us goodbye.

"We'll get him next time," I tell Asher, only to find his attention is rooted on the staff I'm holding across his chest.

"You've had your specter this entire time?" he seethes, the gold in his irises brightening. "Why didn't you say that in the first place?!" Snatching it from my hands, Asher retreats a few steps from the edge and glowers at me. I shrug, flicking my hand into his gut.

"Thought you could use the cardio," I bite back a smile. The anger flees Asher's scarred face and for a brief moment, we let the atmosphere soften between us. It occurs to me, I haven't smiled or enjoyed anyone's company in weeks. Possibly months, as each day blurs into the next and my situation only seems to get worse. "Come on, let's catch this bastard and give him an extra beating for the run-around before you reap the shit outta him." Asher smiles now, a full-toothed grin that looks out of place among his otherwise scarred and reddened features.

"You know what, Hoax. I'm starting to like the way you think."

A blast of heat pulls me from my reclined position on the charred grass outside Hell's gates and directly into a plush living area. I'd been power-sparring with Asher and Hog-Face until they were called away to do some actual work. I have no issues calling to my power down there, probably because Hell is where I'm supposed to be. Stretching the limits of the purple electric I can whip, shoot and swirl is beyond refreshing - like rediscovering myself when I'd been wandering in the abyss. Following those I loved around and accepting that's all I would be good for anymore.

Shooting upright, the modern suite falls away when my sights become centered on the two males standing near a dining area. Pyro's eyes are ablaze in his head, his hair pure flame as he grits his teeth and clutches a glass capsule between his steaming hands. Blue and orange fire pierces the chamber, swirling against the glass in a captivating and worrying display. The most worrying part is the man leering over Pyro's smile, a shit-eating grin spread across his unwrinkled face. Christopher.

Pyro is clearly too distracted to realize the way Christopher's chest and shoulders are filling out his suit too snuggly. Or how there's no sight of his cane, not that his meaty thighs in those slacks would need one. The hair on his head is thickening, the dark roots still growing strong. Those watchful blue eyes watch Pyro's flames too closely, the tilt in his lips spreading unease in me.

Within the canister and drawing all of our attention, a figure becomes visible through the flames. A tiny woman, dancing like a gypsy and using the flames as her sashes. She twirls happily, her fiery hair swaying back and forth like the waves of the ocean. Right up until an audible click locks the capsule and cuts her off from Pyro. Halting her rhythmic movements, she visibly panics. Banging her tiny fists on the inside, pressing her fingers on the glass as she tries to reconnect to the male she's been a part of. It occurs to me then who the figure is, and exactly what Pyro has shaped his entire existence and ability around - Mania.

Chuckling, Christopher presses a button on his phone and within an instant, two guards storm from the elevator. They pluck the capsule from Pyro's numb hands, the figure inside wrapping her arms around herself and sinking to her knees. Turning to leave with his guards, Christopher doesn't spare Pyro another look until my friend lashes out and grabs his arm.

"What about Ghost?" he asks. My gut drops then and alarm bells ring in my head. What the hell is happening with Ghost? Christopher reaches for the TV control, actively twisting from Pyro's weakened grip and tells him to switch to a channel on the screen. Raw hatred bleeds through my dead being, fully focused on the man who is playing us all like pieces on a chess board. Halting in the elevator, Christopher twists an evil smile back into the suite.

"-and Pyro. Thanks for your donation to my cause. I have the ideal candidate to benefit from your generous gift." Anger sweeps through me, my arms crackling with the burst of swirling purple energy encasing them. I'm ready to take this fucker down, but then my eyes slide to Pyro's and all I find there is defeat. Not the male I thought would have been ready to tear this building down, but someone who is utterly lost at sea without a life raft. Pyro drops in the armchair, his eyes a dimmer shade of red and limbs hanging limply by his side. That's it.

Leaving my brother to wallow in self-pity, I stride through the elevator doors just after they close. The guards kneel in unison, securing the glass capsule in a padded briefcase. They are wearing similar suits to their boss, black with white shirts buttoned up to the jawline. Even have the shades like an old-fashioned cop movie. Fancy music plays from hidden speakers and the smug grin on Christopher's face doesn't falter the entire forty-five levels down to the ground floor. Exiting the elevator, I remain uncomfortably close with one goal in mind. Do not let that briefcase out of my sight.

The guards round to Christopher's front, blocking him from the hordes of humans that notice he has entered the lobby. Like a celebrity is in their midst, they surge forward, calling and begging for his attention. The dulled ambers of a setting sun surround the glass front of the hotel, sparking the glittering dresses and diamond jewelry in its dying glow. Each man is in an obnoxious suit, the trophy wife on their arm smiling and flicking around a piece of paper. A betting ballot, if my eyes adjust quick enough. Waving them off, Christopher's shining loafers don't falter as he strides straight to the main doors - a man on a mission.

A limo pulls up as soon as he breaches the balmy evening air, the back door swiftly opened by one of the guards. Passing him the briefcase, the guard lowers his head obediently and allows his boss to slide into the cab without even a grunt of appreciation. I nudge in after him, the door rudely being slammed on my transparent leg. All traces of the pleasant man Christopher just presented to his fans has vanished without a trace of return. Instead, a sinister old man sits beside me, his fingers drumming on the briefcase impatiently.

The limo rolls forward with ease, navigating the winding roads connecting the row of hotels. I peer out of the window, beyond Christopher's shadowed scowl, to get my first glimpse of exactly where I am or what's happening here. The hotels create a continuous circle around a giant crater in the Earth. I can't see what's down below, but the tiny metal fence separating the road from the verge isn't saving anyone. Fragments of my thoughts piece together and I recall standing in the open arena, staring up at the hotels high above. Damn. Mania and Ghost are down there, with fuck knows what else.

Without once increasing its casual speed, the limo soon stops in front of a hotel that matches the last one perfectly. For all I know, we could have gone in a circle and returned to the same place if it weren't for the heightened security posted outside the double glass doors. Responding to the order in their earpieces, bulky guards push open the gold handles while the others urge guests to stand back. They all pull out their phones, flashing quick photos as Christopher edges out of the cab and raises a polite hand to them all.

"Good evening everyone," he smiles fakely. "Enjoy your evenings. Tomorrow brings another day of entertainment you can't find anywhere else." The crowd cheers for Christopher's practiced words that I can imagine are on a flyer somewhere. A path is created by the security's broad chests, welcoming Christopher and his two loyal lackeys beneath the ostentatious chandelier and gold fixtures dripping from every wall. A bar is visible to the right, filled with huge flat screens above betting tables. Dead ahead, an elevator is situated in the same place as the last hotel which I imagine leads to the guest rooms on the above levels. Christopher, however, diverts at the last moment and ascends a grand staircase that curves around the back of the shaft and out of the general public's eyeline.

Tracking the gold railing, a secret elevator becomes visible but that's not Christopher's destination. Instead, he passes the briefcase to one of his guards and tells him to take it to the lab, then diverts into a room behind a door only accessible by a retinal scanner. I find myself torn, my eyes watching the briefcase disappear in the elevator yet Christopher's actions are my concern. Whatever the bastard is up to, I need to know.

Stepping through the door, I find myself in a surveillance room, screens postured up on every inch of the opposite wall. A few men and a woman sit on wheeled chairs, sliding across the wooden floor between the multiple keypads laid out across the counter that stretches from wall to wall. More interesting than that, a pair of Mutes are slumped in the corner, their heads knocking together and eyes closed. By the match in their features and size, I'd hazard a guess at them being twins. Suction pads are attached to each of their temples, connecting them to a huge machine with intertwined wires.

The machine whirs and flashes, seeming to pulse off their very heartbeats.

"How are we doing?" Christopher asks, paying no mind to the Mutes. He stands behind the woman, pressing his hands down on her backrest so she can't move the chair.

"Everything's working as it should. The Minotaur's door has been released with the order you requested. The highest rankers have just received their latest aids and the drones are managing to catch all the action in full HD." She looks up at Christopher uneasily, waiting for him to release her chair so she can get back to work.

"Very good. You can release our Ghost-ly friend from the rec room now," Christopher grunts and I frown. The man to his left scoots across to a keyboard, his fingers flying over the keys as I look at the screen he's focused on. Ghost is hunched over his own knees, crumpled on the ground and huffing in boredom. The torch on the wall of what I would call a cave, not a rec room, flickers across his milky white eyes and stark hair. Out of view, a door must open because Ghost's face flicks upwards, and a moment later he pulls himself up to his feet. All the while, the Mutes seemingly asleep or tranced in the corner frown in concentration, their eyeballs fluttering behind closed lids.

Pleased with what he can see across the screens, whereas all I see are Mutes creeping around in the dark hunting for a safe place to hide, Christopher turns to leave and pauses in the doorway.

"Ahh, before I forget. I need an aid delivered to Mania. A promise I made in exchange for a gift I needed, and I'm nothing if not a man of my word," he sneers. I loathe him with everything in my being and if looks could kill, I'd have incinerated him where he stands.

"What aid would you like? A first aid kit, food supplies, a weapon?"

"Oh no, nothing helpful. Send her..." he looks around and then pulls out his wallet. Every slot is filled with a replica of the same key card, black with a detailed silver pattern disappearing into the leather. "One of these, with compliments from me. Add the inscription, *Find the exit where it all began.*"

"You want to send her a key card to the asylum that she won't be able to use?" the woman asks, swiveling in her chair with a frown.

Christopher stands taller and she suddenly looks down, sensing she's overstepped.

"Do you have a problem with that?" The woman shakes her head and accepts the key card. Avoiding Christopher's hard stare, she walks to the cabinet across the room and pulls out a drawer filled with gold gift boxes, complete with red satin bows. After waiting for her to place the item inside one and start scrawling his message on a piece of card, he leaves without another word. This time, he does take the elevator and just as my foot steps over the threshold to follow, a sudden scream in my ears tears me away.

Blinking, I come face to stone with a cracked wall like those in the labyrinth. A vine lashes out, sensing my presence yet its thorned length whips through my spirit and retreats back limply in defeat. I look around, trying to sense what called me here but there's nothing. Uneven slabs creating the rocky terrain from one dead end to the other. The faint buzz of drones circling, hunting for action worth televising. Under the light of the moon, I wander around until morning dawns, passing through walls and arenas, searching for a glimpse of Ghost or Mania. For a maze of Mutes and seemingly nowhere to hide, there's no one around. That doesn't bode well for our kind.

Strolling around the corner, pretending I can kick at the rocks in my way, I halt at the curious sight ahead. Mania's red and black hair shifts gently with her measured steps, following a male I've never seen before. I shift my angle, spotting a vine wrapped around her skeletal hand. The other end is tied to the male's wrist, his eyes sliding back with humor filling their pale pink depths. Drawing to a stop in front of a dead end, he yanks at the restraint Mania was supposed to have on him and opens a sliding door, urging her to walk inside.

"Don't fucking do it," I mutter beneath my breath, rushing to catch up. Whoever this asshole is, I don't know or trust him. Or the dead bird clutched in his free hand. Mania tries to back up but the male slides an arm around her body, caging her against him. White hot rage blinds me at the sight of him touching her. His mouth near her ear, his grin growing with bad intentions.

On the next step I take, the ground cracks beneath my shoe. A zigzag curves through the Earth, hunting for the fucker that touched my girl. He drops Mania and like a true gentleman, ditches her and flees into the cave. Closing her out, Mania turns just before the ground opens up and swallows her whole. My heart lurches into my mouth as I dive into the pit I created and run to drop down by her side. A drone lowers at that moment, reveling in Mania's pain as she screams, gripping her knees to her chest. A further rumble ripples down the cavern, one that wasn't caused by me. I think.

"Mania, you need to move," I beg her, soothing my hands over her face. Fuck, I wanted to save her. Not hurt her.

"I...can't..." Mania replies, her voice cracking on a sob she can't retain. Rolling onto her front, she leans her forehead on the ground to avoid the drone's intrusion. I don't even question how or why she can hear me now, only thankful that she can.

"Mania," I order with more vigor this time. Rolling her head to the side, she flinches as if she can see me and jerks upright on her knees. Drawing her into my arms, I hesitate long enough for a brief hug before the tunnel's tremors turn thunderous. It's definitely not me this time. Something is coming.

Shifting my spirit to the other end of the passage, I search for a sign of what to expect. Curving around the next alley, the crack stretches past where I recently appeared, leaving nothing but a mere ridge high above. Seeming to never end, I frown back to Mania when I finally see what we're contending with. Fire. Not like Pyro's fire, but a single tendril, slithering from the pits of the Earth behind where Mania still lays. She peers up at me, her blood-red eyes locking on mine once more.

"Move it!" I shout and finally, she listens. Using the wall to aid her,

Mania pushes up to her feet with a wince of pain. Then, she hobbles down the elongated crater, her eyes fixed with mine the entire way. I try to smile in an attempt to reassure her but as the fire rises like a snake centered on his prey, she notes my concern. A pair of fangs stretch from the fiery snake's mouth and it snaps out, just missing Mania who forgets her pain and runs like hell.

I open my arms, desperate to keep her attention on me but it's no use. The snake falls into a raging sea of fire, igniting her pale face as she braves a look back. Raging forward, the flames engulf anything in their way, licking at Mania's heels. She screams a blood-curdling sound that resonates with how I'm feeling. Bringing her red eyes back to this way, I see the determination to get to me. And dammit, I believe myself that I can save her. I can teleport her anywhere else, remind her of my oath to protect her. She's so close now, I can see the tears leaking from her eyes and as she dives forward, sailing through the air, I close my arms around her beautifully damaged body.

She sails straight through me, her head connecting with the wall behind. I drop down, pulling on whatever power will respond to help me ease the swelling on her already cracked skull. Typically, nothing happens so I quell my guilt by curling up on the ground, trying to cradle her sleeping body. The fires hang back, as if they're being controlled by an unknown force. As if they don't really want to hurt Mania, just scare her.

Drawing my knuckles over her porcelain face, I take a moment to admire her beauty. Even with the additions of her human form, she's perfect to me. The blackness of her lips. The crack lining her forehead and the dark circles edging around her long eyelashes. If I'd known what she's come to mean to me, I wouldn't have hesitated from the first moment we met. I knew then she was special, but I should have realized that's because she was meant for me. And Pyro, and Ghost. She united us, even when I'd become disconnected to the male they knew me as. I just wish I could have had more time in her life.

A deep breath flutters from Mania's parted lips, and slowly, she begins to fade. It's gradual at first, like she's simply being drawn into her surroundings. But then I realize she's not the one becoming distant - it's me. I'm being pulled away from her, despite my determination to stay. When my newfound and unstable force doesn't answer my call, I blink uselessly, as if that will keep her in my sight. However, by the time my eyelids have flicked shut and reopened, I'm no longer in the labyrinth.

"He's here," a male calls and all heads swing my way.

"Welcome Hoax," Christopher smiles menacingly just over my shoulder, in what appears to be the Afterlife Asylum's lab. Every head in the room follows the eyeline of the Detective, their task forgotten to greet me with tight smiles. I'm under no illusion they can't actually see me, but the mute from the train tunnels is my giveaway. A couple of MRA agents are posted around the huge cylinder I recognize all too well, ignoring whatever poor creatures are trapped inside the other tanks.

Even without my senses, the clinical scent of the laboratory washes over me. A lengthy tank I know all too well stands tall near the back of the room. I stroll closer, unable to look away, even though the sight is nauseating. Amber-colored liquid surrounds my physical body as tubes disappear into my skin, melding with my cable tattoos. Above a mask covering half of my face, my indigo hair shifts weightlessly.

"Move towards the tank," the male voice comes again. The same one who announced my arrival and is leaning against a computer station to my right. A pair of burning gold eyes pierce my spirit, and even though the scientists gravitate towards the Mute from the train tunnels, he doesn't seem interested in interacting. The Detective pushes a hand through his blue-tipped hair, straightening a leather jacket he seems much more at ease in.

"He's in a stable condition. Tests indicate no sign of abnormalities and vitals are as expected. We're awaiting your order to implement the eternal flame, Sir." A woman steps forward, clutching her clipboard with her chest pushed out proudly. Batting long lashes at Christopher from beneath her thickly-rimmed glasses, a badge on her lab coat marks her as Lead Engineer. Engineer of my fate, it would seem. The center of the room hosts a lengthy table covered in files and printed pages of data.

"Excellent," Christopher grins. Like a class-A asshole, he pulls up a wheeled leather chair and takes a seat as if about to watch his favorite circus act. It doesn't surprise me when a young man in a lab coat too long for him rushes over to place a cigar and cutter on the desk nearby. All ready for the pioneering pat on the back Christopher is about to receive for his capturing and experimentations. The worst part is, it's not even illegal. The Mutes have no rights, no protection and no future. "Everyone to your stations."

Assistants in lab coats rush around the cylinder, hastily tapping touchpads on the side or checking stats on the closest monitor. One blonde in particular types furiously on a keypad and the same pull that drew me here tugs at my spirit again. Bubbles float through a tube that is attached to the oxygen mask covering my face. Flicking my eyes back and forth, I understand what's happening but my mind either refuses to believe it or my thought process is struggling to keep up.

"All systems go," the blonde swivels in her chair to face Christopher. He lifts a hand, beckoning a nearby team over with a flick of two fingers. The five men who respond aren't dressed in lab coats or carrying clipboards around for show. Navy blue fatigues cling to their muscled bodies, machine guns strapped to their fronts. As a unit, they follow the silent order to heave the capsule from the table they were crowding around and walk over to the tank. Pyro's fires.

Fires lick the sides of the glass, swirling in a continuous pattern of red, yellow and orange. That's not the most beautiful part though. In the center, a fiery female figure rolls her hips side to side, dancing in the midst of the chaos. Blue tints float through her flowing hair and spiral around her limbs. Just like before, I find myself captivated, following the cylinder right up until the end cap is loosened and the team push it into a hole at the base of my tank with choreographed movements.

My eyes widen as it all clicks into place. A mixture of elation and dread settles within me, wanting this to be the end of my silent suffering but also knowing it would only be the beginning of a different kind. The Detective stands on a grunt, his eyes starting to glow gold and drawing Christopher's irritated attention.

"Something the matter?" he bites, clearly wanting no further interruption in his scheming. The Detective strolls forward in my direction, his hand swiping the air and just brushing through my inked arm.

"I sense something else," he mumbles, cocking his head with his luminescent eyes traveling across the lab for the source of his 'detection.'

"You know your ability becomes erratic when I'm around, and there's Mutes in most of the tanks. Sit back down and let us continue," Christopher orders. Swiveling back in his chair, he sighs heavily and lifts a head high in the air. "Proceed." All at once, scientists with glimmering chrome keys push them into slots at their computer desks and turn to the right. Buttons light up across the boards, which they press in unison. Multiple things happen then, some too fast to track the order while panic surges forth in my gut.

A hiss sounds, like that of a pressure value opening and I watch the scientists push various vials into the machines that house the mass of wires leading to my body. Once safely inside, they close the hatches and lock them before giving who I'll presume is the head scientist a solid thumbs up. She's the woman who spoke before, still clutching at her clipboard to rapidly take notes.

The dense, orange liquid in the tank bursts to life with a vibrant glow. Machines whirl, the tubes entering my body fill with a range of different mixtures while the thick cord spearing my chest is connected directly to the fiery cylinder. Flames race into my physical body, which jolts back from the sheer force of impact. At the same time, a crater of light penetrates my spirit form. It's blinding, forcing me to squint. Tearing through my chest, I uselessly try to cover the fractures and among it all, I catch a glimpse of piercing blue eyes. Christopher is watching my physical body jerk around inside the tank with such unadulterated glee, one single thought filters through my mind. I can't re-enter the world on Christopher's terms.

As quickly as it began, the spotlight in the tank shuts off. The liquid gushes out through thick pipes, draining until every last drop has gone and my body is laying slumped on the base. The wires invading my body detach, slithering away from my skin and back into the nearby computers they are connected to.

A gasp is torn from my spirit unexpectedly, the light fading to reveal a gaping hole through the center of my chest. I try to cover it, but my hands are fading too. Dropping to my knees, I scrunch my eyes, trying to picture anywhere else to teleport to. But then, maybe this is all part of the process. Maybe I could be holding Mania by the end of the day, in that crazed maze or not. I'd find her. A moment of silence passes while everyone waits. Even me, hunched over and clutching my chest while the Detectives eyes burn hotter in my direction.

Suddenly, the fires explode inside the tank. Roaring upwards, they swirl and beat against the inside of the glass, completely consuming my body. Torn between my instinct to flock into the tank and run from it, the fires lash out again, a dominant display of royal blue. At the base of the tank, my body is a mere shadow, lost to the mercy of Pyro's flames. A fresh wave of pain storms through my spirit in a way I haven't felt before. It's internal and all consuming, any hope of reuniting with my brothers and Mania beginning to drift away.

Closing my eyes, I try to focus on her face, willing my spirit to put as much distance as possible between me and my body. When the excited chatter and whirring machines cause too much of a distraction to permit that, I turn my efforts to resist the urge. The blissful promise of peace that if I re-enter my body, I'll almost be whole again. I won't need my consciousness to know Mania, to hold her, soothe her, kiss her. But anything orchestrated by Christopher will inevitably go wrong. He'll no doubt use me as his personal puppet and keep a tight hold of my strings. So for that reason, I fight.

Drawing on the dregs of my will, the power simmering under the surface responds instantly in my time of need. A purple glow coats my spirit, welling me up from the inside. I rise to my feet, turn away from my physical form and take a strained step in the other direction. Then another, through the immense pull trying to yank me backwards.

The sound of a heartbeat suddenly pulsing through the room almost breaks me. A steady, rhythmic beat that belongs to me. Not a room of scientists and reinforcements. Not a ruthless psychopath and his minions. Forcing another foot forward, the purple glow around me brightens and with a sudden clench of my fists, the bond snaps. A relieved smile graces my lips, although my elation is short-lived. The thump of a strong heart is still pulsing through the speakers, along with Christopher's malicious chuckle and slow hand clap. And that's when I thoroughly lose my shit.

Throwing my arms wide, purple cannon balls of pulsing electric bursts from my fingerless palms, spiraling straight into the cylinder. The glass tank detonates, spraying glass everywhere. While the others duck for cover, I regretfully backtrack on the distance I'd manage to create, needing to see. Needing to know before I disappear if it was worth it.

The flames are still reaching high into the air, snapping at anyone who is too close. Beginning to churn like a tornado, I meet the base of the tank to see myself curled up in the center. Reaching out, I push my arm through the wall of flame. The instant I connect with my true self, the fires are sucked into my body and completely absorbed. Other than the faint reddish twinge to my veins, it is as if they were never here at all.

My spirit on the other hand, has completely restored itself, yet it's still here. I'm still here. Worrying the experiment didn't work, I stare at myself, hunting for signs of life. Christopher has the same idea, rushing forward to shove me onto my back.

"We did it!" he announces, causing the rest of the audience around the tank to burst into applause. I barely hear them though, all noise muffled out by the pair of glowing purple eyes staring directly at me. From behind the mask covering my face, my physical form breathes deeply as he takes his first measured blink.

"Not quite," the Detective appears at Christopher's side, his stone-cold voice breaking through the cheering and glowing eyes focused on me. "His spirit is still here. He hasn't crossed over as intended." All clapping halts.

"Mmmm," Christopher hums in the back of his throat, scratching at his chin thoughtfully. Easing my body up, the asshole who is now a mirror image of his mad scientist relative unclasps the oxygen mask on my face and eases it off. It's eerie seeing myself move, watching my eyes drift across the observing crowd. When I was hanging limply like Houdini's puppet, it was easier to detach myself from the fact I'm both present in the real world and not there at the same time. Now, with disjointed movements and a blank stare, I'm dreading what kind of Frankenstein version of myself they're revived. With a slight nod, Christopher beams and looks at his bodyguards watching from a safe distance.

"Fetch Brainwash. I don't care how much it costs, we need his services immediately." Nodding, the pair head for a landline telephone on the far wall together and my spirit thunders with dread. What the fuck is Brainwash going to do to me? At one of the lab assistant's request, an MRA agent grabs one of my arms each and hoist me to my feet. All the while, my body doesn't react, resist, fight back. Nothing. I'm no better than a drone.

"Did you hear me, Sir?" the lead scientist approaches tentatively, peering over her clipboard. "The spirit is still separated, possibly for good now." Pulling himself upright and dusting off his suit jacket, Christopher's grin looks like it's permanently etched onto his face.

"No matter. We have what we needed and this might be the best outcome. A body I can mold, a brain I can re-program but a spirit is no use to me. Not when we're this close to achieving what we set out to do."

I stagger back through the curious crowd when it all becomes too much, needing to put space before me and, well...me. My head is swimming with questions and confusion, and all I want to do is get the fuck out of here. Whatever they're doing or intend to have me do, I don't want to know. Yet I'll have to know. Every horrid, regretful detail because this is my fault. My choice. I've rendered myself without a body, and more importantly, without a way to return.

HOAX

CHAPTER TEN

"Asher!" I scream at the top of my lungs. I didn't know what else to do or where to go. My boots land heavily on the charred grass at Hell's front door, the iron entrance stretching high above. Mutated figures drip from the gates in the same rusted metal, their jaws unhinged and open on frozen screams. From here, I can feel the force of Hellfire beyond a series of stone archways. The fire blazes all the way from the ground to the endless sky, its roar swallowing the agonizing scream of its latest victim. Hog-Face is strolling past the inside, appearing just as the guard on duty tries to wrestle me into the line of prisoners. Fat chance.

"Hoax?" he snorts, diverting from his course to exit via the opening between the two gates. His tusks are cast in shadow as he faces out into the darkness, the fiery glow surrounding him like a stormy halo. "How did you get down here without a scepter?"

"I just...teleported, I guess. Like I do everywhere. But it doesn't matter right now. I need Asher, I need to-" I lift my hands in exasperation, not knowing where to finish that sentence. I don't even know what urged me to come here, but when there's only one place you can actually interact with others, it seemed like my only option.

"I've got this Gerald," Asher appears, tapping his demon associate on the shoulder. *Gerald?* I muse to myself. That doesn't suit Hog-Face at all. The demon shrugs and briskly waves goodbye, leaving me in a weird stand-off against Asher's flame-filled eyes. His shoulders are bunched, his stance too straight while the lava in his face bubbles and spits.

"What's happened?" Asher grits out, although I sense I'm not the only one with problems currently. Scrubbing a hand over my face, I turn on a groan and then spin straight back.

"These other astral planes of yours. Anywhere we can grab a drink?" I settle on, deciding for one second in my damn existence, I'm going to be a *normal* guy. It seems that even before I died, I had no life worth of remembering. If I truly am cut off from my body, Mania and the living world, I might as well settle for having a respite from the anguish of it all. Asher watches me carefully, his impassive expression not faulting while the moment stretches on. The clink of chains, occasional sob from a prisoner and scream grate on my subconscious, the heat settling uncomfortably on my skin.

"I know a place," Asher finally nods. Clicking his fingers, the scepter I left him with in the maze appears in his hand. In a rush of grabbing my shoulder and tapping it on the ground, we morph into a world that is anything but human. The scent of a recent fall of rain and churned grass tingles my nostrils as I inhale deeply, noting the rhythmic beating inside my chest. I press a hand over the motherboard circuit inked across my heart with the hint of a skull's face peering out from beneath and gasp.

"I'm...alive?!" I ask, a choked giggle escaping my lips. Filled with a light-headed sense of giddiness, I punch Asher in the arm and run among the grass. Lifting my arms out wide like I might take off in flight, I veer around, the haze of a blue and green landscape speeding past my eyes. The tiny blades lick at my skin when I drop down, rolling in the dew. Laughter continues to stream from my mouth as I let go and revel in this feeling. The sensation of fresh air filling my lungs, the wash of a crisp breeze touching my body. A shadow looms over me as Asher kicks my ribs.

"Thought you wanted a drink, not to moon bathe." I peer up, past the face that's missing the rivets of scars, to see a pair of moons hanging in a star-ridden sky. The pearlescent orbs are faded, framing a star as bright as the sun in the center. Asher hoists me up but I can't take my eyes off the sparkling stars against the pale blue of day. Clouds roll by a rocky mountain range claiming the horizon, stretching high in competition with each other across the rolling green fields. A shimmering river curves from by mine and Asher's feet towards a building of vertical glass shards. Similar structures appear among the mountains, glinting like clusters of upside-down icicles.

"Where the fuck are we? And why am I alive, and what happened to your scars?" I ask all at once, not able to settle on a question. Asher's boots begin to move, leaving me to trail behind. Holding the specter high from the ground doesn't stop various shades and styles of flowers stretching up to stroke the wood, perhaps sensing the magic emitting from it.

"An alternative to reality," is the only answer I receive. Running to catch up, I find a skip in my step and my past worries have ebbed away. What even were they? By the time I come level to peer at Asher's un-smoking beard, there's a small smirk planted there. We walk in a comfortable silence until a pathway of white pebbles appears from the grass and leads towards the ice structure ahead. As we approach, I see it's not glass or ice, but rather, gemstones. Tall as statues, the jewels create a formidable exterior around a rounded, white door. Asher doesn't knock, twisting the gold handle and permitting himself entry with me close behind.

The inside is just as stunning, from its opulent shimming white wallpaper with hints of gold that reflect off a diamond chandelier. Best of all, it's a bar. Gliding over the polished floor, my fingers skate over the white, leathered backrests of empty seats framing glass tables. The bar itself is an array of colored diamonds, encased in an elongated slab of resin. Asher takes a seat on a stool, patting for me to join him as a man rounds from an archway leading out back.

"Well, well. I wasn't expecting company today. Where have you boys come from?" The way he says 'boys' would usually have irritated me but instead, a stupidly large smile stretches across my face and at one point, my tongue lolls to hang out.

"Hell, on a different astral plane," Asher drums his fingers in a pattern over to me and bobs me on the nose. I chuckle, bumping into his side. "Hoping for a drink and a good time."

"That, I can do," the male smiles. Focusing my eyes, which seem to have a glaze coating them I can't blink away, I see he's about my height and also lean in build, yet his coloring reflects his ice-palace perfectly. Stark white hair stands on end, similar to Ghost's but almost translucent to match hollowly pale eyes. His skin has a pale blue twinge, like he's coated in a layer of frost. Reaching for two crystal glasses from the back shelves, he plucks out a bottle of vibrant blue liquid. Crushed ice trapped inside the bottle clinks against the sides as he pours us both a decent measure.

Sliding them across the bar, a hint of pink catches my gaze. It's small and faint, yet when it's the only source of color against a sea of white, I narrow my eyes in curiosity. When his arm tries to retreat, I snatch his wrist and drag him forward until my face is practically on his shoulder.

"Who is this?" I smile. A creature about the size of my thumb shifts side to side, pink and plump like a worm, yet with his features of a shrimp. Legs ripple down its fleshy body to a fin-like tale, a pair of beady eyes peering at me beneath an extended antennae that tickles my cheek. It's cute, in a chubby, slimy and wriggly kind-of-way.

"This here is Marina. She keeps me company during the long days. It's rare for us to have such fine visitors." I nod at his compliment and sip the blue drink. Fruity liquor skates across my tongue and I groan. I'm in heaven. The first flavor to tantalize my taste buds since my tongue last delved into Mania's mouth, something I long to have again if it kills me.

Laughter bubbles from my throat, mixed with a hiccup as I slide from the stool and find a leather-backed chair instead.

"Wanna share the joke?" Asher asks, spinning with a grin like he's already in on it. I wave him away, preferring to slump back and let my eyes drift closed. I've opted for the seat in front of an open fireplace and kick off my shoes to push my toes into a plush rug. Fuck, it's so much softer than I even imagined.

Scrunching up my toes and rolling my ankles around in the white fur, I muse at the flames of the fire. Something tugs at my chest but I ignore it in favor of wondering how a house made of ice doesn't melt with an open roaring fire. But it's not like it's important. Nothing is anymore. Lifting the glass to my lips, I try to savor every last drop of the liquid, swishing it around my mouth before swallowing slowly.

"I used to be a Mute too, you know," Asher sways on his stool. His smile stretches wide across his scars. Lifting the drink in my direction, he downs the liquid and hands it back for a refill. "A damn good one." Raising my glass in solidarity, the questions tumbling through my mind don't find their voice. Or my voice? Whatever.

Placing the tumbler down, I misjudge the low height of a nearby table and it drops, spinning onto the surface and spilling the rest of the contents. Fuck it. My fingers trail the length of the leather seat beneath me, pushing down the wooden leg almost sensually. It's been so long since I've felt anything too. I find a cool relief in the hard surface and dip my nail in and out of the screw's grooves, humming to myself.

What a fine life this is. I reckon I could hide out back with a creepy little companion and never leave too, if this were my home. Hell, maybe it could be. It doesn't look like there's any others waging war on all that rolling real estate outside. Asher and I could build our own cabin out of wood, sweat and forgotten problems. All that'd be missing is…hang on. What was it I wanted? Or maybe it was a who?

"I can be whoever you want," the husky voice breathes into my ear, steadily raising in pitch. A figure rounds the back of my chair from seemingly nowhere, swinging a leg over my lap to settle a pair of slender hips there. No, not slender - skeletal. The porcelain white skin of her face is marred by black lips and red eyes, framed by lengths of silky waves in the same colors. A winged skull tattoo shifts upon her chest with each breath, above a leather and lace corset that makes my heart pound. The curve of her breasts are so close to my face and as her arms wind around my neck, I merely drop my head to lie there. Listening to her heartbeat, reveling in the warmth she's been missing. Wait, why was it missing?

A faint memory trickles through my bliss-filled thoughts, of shivering hands around a coffee cup. Curled up knees in holey tights. A broken heart and shattered resolve. Shaking my head, the mistress of death in my lap tilts up my chin, one corner of her lips shifting into a smirk.

"It's okay Hoax. I'm here, and I'm all yours." Her pleading tone is my undoing, my cock steadily becoming solid behind the zipper of my cargos. I remember now - that's all I've wanted. To have her, to hold her and worship every inch of her body. To show her what love is supposed to feel like and to share her with…

"Wait," I frown, removing my chin from her gentle fingers. "Where's Pyro and Ghost?"

"Who?" the minx in my lap asks, trying to lean in to kiss away my troubles but I dodge her.

"Pyro and Ghost. We should be together, all of us," I argue. Alarm bells sound in my mind, the noise trying to be drowned out but Asher's sexual moans and bitter laughter. This isn't right. I push her off my lap, standing to tower over the fake Mania. I don't know how I even feel for the trick in the first place, yet the glass slipping blue liquid onto the floor draws my attention.

"Don't be like that Hoax. I know you want me, just take me." Lifting her arms, she tries to draw me close but I step away.

"No." Hearing my rejection, the figure before me shifts and grows until I'm facing the bartender who served me the drink. An angry V sits between his snow-white eyebrows, the blue twinge to his skin growing brighter.

"If you didn't want me," his voice changing from an echo of Mania's to the deep baritone of his own, "then why did you come here?" The brightness of the room darkens, as if the sun outside is being blocked. A cold wind whips around the room, knocking Asher off the female he's mounted across the bar. He drops to the ground, smashing a few stools on his way down, with a pained grunt. The woman left panting sexually on the bar writhes, contorting and shrinking before my eyes until the fleshy form of the worm-shrimp is all that's left.

Asher shoots up on a curse, preparing to beat the shit out of me for interrupting him until his blazing eyes settle on the bar. The worm-shrimp raises a front leg in a wave and Asher slowly bends, reaching for the scepter and never taking his eyes off the creature. Twirling it around his hand, I anticipate the moment he slams the end of the staff down to squish the mini creature, grabbing for his waist and the connection with the bar sparks another teleportation. Leaving the guttural roar of the Mutant shifter behind, we land in the familiar stone surrounding of the maze, staring at the hotel-rimmed sky.

"The next time you feel like going for a drink, take someone else," Asher groans on his back and with another soft tap, he's gone. Nothing to worry about there; I think it's safe to say my days of drinking are solidly over.

I stumble from one astral plane to the next, each footstep landing me in a new destination. Staying clear of Hell, I pass through Rosefield graveyard, the train station, the desert of sand tornados. Each time I seem to return to the labyrinth as if that's where I should be, but I'm no use to anyone there. Watching Mania suffer from the other side of the void separating us is pure torture. Worse than anything awaiting me beyond the gates of Hell when Asher is finally ready to claim his end of our deal.

Because that's quickly becoming my only option. My body may have been revived, but only to become a puppet for Christopher to enjoy pulling my strings. This version of me, the one who longs to joke with my brothers and feel the soft lips of my heart's desire, is doomed to walk the Earth alone. Watching from the sidelines, yearning from the shadows until I finally give up and let myself be reaped.

So instead, I just keep walking and shifting through space. I happen across places I can't remember visiting but maybe my subconscious knows better than I do. A street being tarmacked, an old bakery. Even the crooked house at the end of the street with a sign for

Hermitage Home for Boys outside, all over until I peer up to see the oppressive laboratory staring back at me.

There's no one of significance present, not even my own body. Just a few scientists in lab coats, mostly female, pottering between the other cylinders and taking notes. I follow a mousey girl with freckles the same color as her chocolate brown hair, peering into the tanks to see what's interesting her. The liquid inside each is a similar orange to what mine was, yet the beings aren't recognizable to me. The oxygen masks don't help, leaving just a hint of neon hair here and distinctive tattoos there.

She finishes checking vitals and writing down statistics when a door at the back of the room bursts open. I hadn't noticed there was another exit than the elevator shaft, but the hordes of MRA agents piling into the room prove otherwise. In the center, a pair of Mutes present themselves in similar fatigues. The one on the left I recognize straight away - the Detective, and the swivel of his glowing eyes has me stepping back behind the closest tank. The other Mute is a huge mountain of a man that I don't believe is part of his ability. The bulk of his traps, the strain of his biceps and rigidness of his movements in the tight uniform speaks of years of training and gym sessions.

"What's going on?" the mousey scientist asks, surprising me with the confidence of her head tilt.

"Perimeter breach at the hotel. Some of our own have betrayed us and are leading Pyro directly for the connecting elevator shaft." It's an MRA agent that speaks, the one at the front with more medals than any other. Medals for the capture and slaughter of my kind, no doubt. At the sound of Pyro's name, I glance to the elevator just as the number on top begins to decrease. Dread consumes me and I panic, calling for the purple coating to surround my hands. Anything to aid my brother in his suicide quest to no doubt save me. If only he knew, he was already too late.

I brace for the number on the top of the elevator to reach zero, but it passes and continues to shift - this time through a sequence of acronyms I don't understand. The agents rush forward, dropping into a formation that leaves a row of riot shields in front and men holding guns behind. The Mute Mountain strides to the side, tucking in just behind a shield that barely covers his thighs.

"Remember to shoot low. We want them all alive. Pyro, and the *traitors*," he growls. Cracking his knuckles, my eyes are too busy flicking between them and the elevator to realize someone has snuck up on me until it's too late.

"Hello Hoax," the Detective grins, appearing behind me as he rounds the tank. His eyes are gold coals, burning a glow above his cruel smile. I've seen him in so many outfits now, I can't tell what his usual style is, but the carefully styled quiff to his blue-tipped hair tells me it's not being an active MRA accomplice. A snitch though I can see that with no qualms. Throwing my fingers out wide, balls of purple power surge into my powers and his all-seeing eyes dip to my sides. "Now I've understood how to sense your spirit, you can't hide from me. And whatever is happening here," he gestures towards my hands, "is only making it easier."

The ping of the elevator arriving sounds then and it's too late. Whatever good intentions I had vanish as the lab is plunged into darkness. The sudden spark of a whip lashes out, encasing my body as I try to make it towards Pyro. I struggle against the binds, falling to my front just as the elevator doors slide open and I see my brother tentatively step out beside Enzo.

"Don't!" I shout, raising my hands. The spark of the whip messes with my power, sending two lightning bolts shooting from my palms and directly into the male's chests. The pair fly backwards, slamming into the females they were protecting and all four crash to the floor. I have my own problems to worry about as my hands remain ignited, my power refusing to simmer down but as the doors begin to shut, I sigh in relief.

Until the mountain Mute moves forward and shoves his boot in the way. Bending over the four slumped on the floor, he covers each one of their mouths in turn. I army crawl forward, ignoring the tug of the Detective on my restraints and manage to get close enough when one of the female's voices dashes all my hopes of saving them.

"Chloroform," she mutters before slumping back limply. The mountain Mute smirks, striding away and leaving the MRA agents to do their job. In this instance, their job is to cram as many of them into the elevator as possible and disappear behind the closing doors.

Turning my focus back to the whip curled around my middle, I shudder with the amount of force it takes to retract the purple energy pulsing from my hands. It's as if none of the training with Asher even happened. Eventually, I'm able to lessen the force claiming my limbs and wield it downward to snap the whip. The Detective stumbles back and I twist to see the mousey scientist standing there with her clipboard, assessing the end of the whip.

"Amazing," she marvels, lifting the limp end with her pen. Electricity snaps at the end, much like an evolved taser cocooned in a cable casing. It slithers and worms around with a mind of its own, trying to snap at my heels while I back away. "Do you think it'll be strong enough to hold Shadow?" The Detective shrugs and tosses the broken whip onto a nearby computer station.

"Should do. This was just a prototype and it knocked Hoax on his ass." Sneering in my direction, I flip up the middle finger, really hoping whatever heat sensing ability he has allows him to see the outline. Kneeling down, the Detective levels his glimmering, golden eyes in my direction.

"Run along now little fish. I'll catch you next time." Growling, I flick out my leg which would have smashed out at least four of this fucker's teeth before I shift into the maze. If they're experimenting on ways to trap my spirit, or whoever this Shadow is, I need to stick close to Mania. Maybe during this 'next time' the Detective promised, Mania will be able to see my outline and know I'm still here with her.

Yet as the crowds rush through my body, hurrying somewhere, I get that dreaded sense everything is about to go to shit. For the hundredth time in the past few months.

"*Mania*," I gasp. Her red and black hair whips around her face, her hand clasped around Ghost's arm as he carries…a child? I don't have time to compute what I'm seeing as the walls around us slide an inch closer together and I suddenly understand the rush. Other Mutes are also gripping Ghost wherever they can, making full use of his ability to shift through the walls. I stay close, not letting them out of my sight now I've latched on. Screams of terror distract Mania too many times, her red eyes fleeting from one Mute to the next. A look of guilt passes her face with each wall they pass through until finally, the final arch way is up ahead.

Ghost bulldozes onwards, oblivious to those who try to grab his shirt in desperate hope of salvation. Unfortunately, their hands slip straight through his body and when the walls inch another notch closer, full-out chaos breaks out. The claws come out, everyone only caring for themselves and as the group spill through the archway, the walls suddenly snap together and silence those who weren't fast enough to make it. Swallowing thickly, I try to block out the warzone I've just entered and take in my surroundings.

Tall, stone walls conceal us in a circular hole in the ground, etched with thorned vines that have a life of their own. Anyone who steps back close enough gets a painful reminder to huddle in the center. There seems to be Mutes everywhere, but on closer inspection, they're all just too frantic to stand still. Between the murmurs of confusion and heads shifting in the way, I spot a podium across the far side of our latest prison. A stage of stone, ten-feet in the air and in the center is my worst nightmare. Still stiff, still staring blankly through a shimmering bubble protecting him. Or me. Christopher sure wasted no time putting my body to good use.

"No fucking way," Ghost breathes, spotting my body the same time Mania does. She takes an automatic step forward, releasing her from the safety of Ghost's ability and unbelievably, my body's head snaps to her. My eyes settle on Mania's so strongly, even from this side of the void separating us, I can feel the tie between the two. He remembers her. Or…and I hate to always be the negative Nancy here, Christopher has had his brain re-programmed to seek her out. I can't imagine the latter comes with good intentions, so for what it's worth, I move to stand in front of Mania protectively.

Oof. Mania flies through my spirit and crashes to the floor by my feet, a body tackling her to stay down. I raise my eyebrows at the display, spotting Pyro's red hair as he surges Mania's torso in a mix of desperation and lust. He tries to remain rigid, keeping his shoulders bunched but the second her eyes settle on his with recognition, the battle is lost. Their lips crash together like a sea pummeling a sinking ship.

Without a trace of jealousy, not like the irritated shudder Ghost fails to suppress anyway, I crouch down to watch. It's like a movie playing out before my eyes, the crest of a happy ending that fills you with the gooey feels. Well, this is even better. My heart's desire being swaddled by the passionate love of her true mate. The pair finally coming together after all this time, to reunite their love and find strength among the chaos. I've watched Mania lose herself for far too long to not approve of this. At least, regardless of what does or doesn't happen to me, I can have the knowledge she won't be alone ever again.

The crackle of a drone lowers overhead, soon followed by the rasp of Christopher's voice to bring my happy fantasy crashing down. Mania and Pyro reluctantly break apart, raising to stand. I follow suit, smirking as Ghost quickly links his fingers with Mania's on Pyro's chest. The logical part of my brain knows it's useless but I let my heart lead for once and copy the action, combining the four of us in my palms. Drowning out Christopher's words as he sends another wave of anarchy through the crowds, I push all my energy into my hands, silently praying the trio might sense me. Not just the man standing on the podium staring down, but my spirit. My soul and the undying love for them all I'll never shake.

Swinging my eyes back to my physical form, ignoring the strange sense of Deja vu I get every time I glance at him, it's becoming clearer he has been programmed to watch Mania. His muscles haven't moved a millimeter, his jaw locked into place and eyes boring into her already cracked skull. The wash of helplessness threatens to consume me when a figure among the crowd gives me pause. He stands out because he's the only Mute with his back turned to the stage, giving me a clear view of his face. An oddly straight moustache, goatie framing his chin and a metal ring in his eyebrow. Motherfucker.

Sensing there's nothing I can do here, I decide trapping this lost fucker and getting back in Asher's good books is possibly the best way to go. Technically it was *him* who led me into an alternate astral plane and allowed himself to nearly fuck a mutating worm-shrimp, but I have a feeling I'm still on his shit-list for it. Maybe this will convince him to aid me with some of his demon power to help Mania, as per our agreement. Stomping after the spirit, he balks and runs for it, leaving a string of curses trailing from my lips.

Leaving Mania in the mostly-capable hands of my brothers, I follow the Mute out of the arena, passing through the walls to stay on his trail. He disappears around a corner and when I move around the same one, I find he's broken into a run and is a fair distance ahead of me. Looks like he either hasn't mastered the art of shifting or he can't. I sigh, moving through the space to appear at the far end in time for him to crash into my chest.

"Nice try, but it's time to take you where you need to be," I tell him as if reading his rights. Grabbing his wrists, I prepare to take us directly to Hell when a body slams into my side. Caught off guard, I tumble off balance and slip through the nearby wall by accident. Appearing back in the narrow alley, I frown at the two faces staring back at me. One, my captive, and the one being a demon. Fully black eyes with no irises look straight through me, all of his visible skin heavily scarred and giving me the vibe this guy died via a grenade to the face.

"This is my soul to reap. You want your own charges, you need to become fully fledged," he grunts, bumping me with his chest in a challenge. I'm not stupid enough to think I could take him one-on-one. I'm a murdered computer geek teethed to the real world. I don't need my memories to know fighting isn't my strong point.

"I was just trying to help out a friend, that's all," I raise my hands. Sure, it'd have been easier to get help via a trade-off but I'm not about to get in the way of this demon's job. That shit's emasculating - mostly for me because the spirit would need to sit back and watch my ass getting handed to me.

"I've heard all about Asher's protégé," the demon snarls and I frown. "Being trained by one of our best doesn't mean you can take whichever assignment you feel like." I take a step forward, intent on asking for clarification but the demon gets the wrong impression. His meaty fist slams into my face a moment later, which apparently includes the row of spikes attached to his knuckles. Searing pain blooms along my jaw, leaving me stunned and clutching my mouth as the demon takes the spirit and leaves. The fuck was all that about?

Drawing my hands away, there's no evidence of blood but the pain doesn't ebb until the sliding archway door opposite lifts and a rush of Mutes skidding out brings a welcome distraction. Mania is visible across the arena, speaking with three versions of the same guy with Pyro flaking her. Ghost is cupping his balls and hobbling over, which doesn't seem out of the ordinary. The guy's a dick at the best of times, makes sense he would get kneed or smacked in it once in a while. Me, however, I did nothing to earn my fat lip and with that thought, I blink and appear in Hell, hunting for answers.

A flash of swirling white energy zooms towards my head as I materialize and manage to duck out the way just in time. Landing on my ass for the second time in a matter of minutes, a full-blown fight rages over head while I scramble to get out of the way. My back crashes into a pair of sturdy, booted legs, their owner plucking me up as if I weigh nothing.

"You shouldn't be here," the cold female voice says, her green eyes not leaving the fight. Any familiarity is a distant memory as she ignores me like I'm no better than the prisoners on the endless chain of shackles. Azella's horns shine with each powerful orb thrown between the two demons, her face set in hard lines with her specter clutched tightly in a clawed hand.

"What's happening?" I ask anyway, not heeding her warning. Maybe I'm out of my league but I've visited enough to know this isn't normal and when Asher is finished, I have a few questions of my own. Widening my legs, I copy Azella's stance with my chest puffed out and the slight hitch in my arms as if braced for an attack. My power works just fine down here so self-defense shouldn't be an issue, I hope.

Before us, on the deadened grass outside Hell's gates, the demon who recently punched me in the face is facing off with a seriously pissed-off Asher.

"Should've stayed out of this, Mantus!" Asher roars, throwing an orb of embers himself. His is black as onyx, almost invisible against the dim background but Mantus is able to dodge it with ease. His own orbs are pure white like deadly snowballs that curve and hunt for their target.

"Hey Newbie," Hog-Face approaches with a rusty old tin or charred popcorn. There's still a rivet of smoke swirling from the burnt remains and as he pushes a hoof of clusters into his mouth, the crunch can be heard over the throwing of orbs. "Want some?" My eyebrows raise and I shake my head, trying to dislodge my cringe when he dips his silver-coated hand back into the bucket.

"I'm good. But I'm not so much a newbie anymore. I've been down here a fair few times."

"As a visitor, maybe. But until you complete the ceremony and have worked for a good ten thousand years, you'll still be considered a newbie. To me anyway."

"What ceremony?" I frown as another ball of white energy barrels this way. Azella moves with the swiftness of a warrior, twirling the staff in her hand to deflect the ball back in the direction it came from. Considering I've seen the orbs hunting down Asher wherever he moves, I'm starting to think Mantus is targeting me on purpose. Drawing on my power to start forming a similar weapon between my hands, Azella delivers a shift smack of the scepter to my shin.

"Stay out of it," she warns again, a threat in her eyes. Turning to Hog-Face, because at least he's not eating me like some outsider, I wait for him to finish a mouthful of popcorn, his tusks dripping drool and nose ring glinting in the occasional light.

"With the utmost respect, tell me what the fuck is going on and don't be cagey about it." Hog-Face chuckles, nudging his head for us to move away from Azella. I comply, hearing her turbans grumble behind me as we move to a small mound in the grassy planes.

Clicking his hoofed fingers together, which I find impressive in itself, a checked blanket appears for us to sit on like we're having a romantic picnic, framed by a display of fireworks. Fireworks that can tear a soul in two and disintegrate whatever remains. Giving up with his hands, Hog-Face shoves his entire snout in the bucket, gobbling up the popcorn and forcing me to wait impatiently.

Asher generates a huge blackened ball between his hands, roaring with the force of catapulting it towards Mantus. It slams him in the chest and much like the first time I met Asher at the cemetery, knocks him flying with a clean hole through the middle of his torso. But Mantus doesn't stay down for more than a few seconds, jumping to his feet as the wound already starts knitting itself back together.

"Mantus is pissed Asher swooped in and stole his special mission to the Devil," Hog-Face grunts, waving a hand between the two. "They've been fighting like this for days and the big guy had enough. He's kicked them both out the gates until one completes the task. Said demon will be welcomed back as the victor and all previous indiscretions will be forgotten. The other has to join the back of the shackle line and return to being a guest in cell block 864,679 for a few thousand years. Spoiler alert," he leans in close enough for his rancid breath to wash over my, "that's where they keep the stretching racks."

Watching the pair throw orbs back and forth in some weird, choreographed version of a fight, questions fly around my head until I pluck one out and decide to start there.

"So, what was the mission?" My indigo eyes meet Hog-Face's muddy brown ones, a surprised grin pulling at his tusked mouth.

"Well, you, of course." A howling cackle leaves the demon beside me and he rolls back and forth on his rounded, pig-like ass.

"Me?" I echo back. "As in, reaping me? Asher and I already have a deal-"

"No, you silly plum. Asher was never sent to reap you. He was sent to *recruit* you. The Devil is always watching and hunting for who has what it takes to become one of us, putting a notch by our names and waiting for us to die. Except, you're still tied to the human world and the Devil is intrigued. The same way I'm curious about how you can teleport without a specter, or stay up there as long as you like." Snapping his chunky fingers, a hot dog smothered in more condiments than meat appears in his hand and he chows it down, as if that revelation hasn't just rocked me off kilt.

"But...you mean," I shake my head. "I can't be a demon. I have to stay on Earth to protect my girl. I have...stuff I need to do and I'm not fully dead, even though I'm invisible to those I care about but... anyways, shouldn't I get a fucking say in what I want to do with the rest of my eternity?" I finally settle on, anger finding cracks in my shock to bleed through. Who is Asher to trick me, to try and define what I'll become without consulting me? He lied to me.

Rising to my feet, I ignore Azella's warning glare and burst an orb of purple energy to life in my hands. With another aggressive shudder, I rip the orb in half and hurl them both at the unexpecting demons. The next one I generate slams into the pair of specters leaning against the decrepit wall leading towards the iron gates. Then, I'm gone.

My feet hit the road in whatever astral plane I've ended up in. I don't care which, as long as it gives me some space from the assholes who will no doubt be tracking me. A gray, empty town sprawls out before me, the sun hidden behind a thick layer of cloud. It doesn't look like any sunshine has ever shone down here away, with wilted flowers laying limp across the pavement. Trees bare of any foliage stand in fenced cylinders, hanging low to scrape my hair with their gnarled fingers. Good to know I'm present in this world before I get a nasty surprise.

The street directs me to a forgotten church in the center of the town. Wooden cladding which was once white is falling from the sanctuary's exterior, exposing holes in the walls to match the caved in roof. The cross above the door is hanging upside down, threatening to crash into the stones steps below. A waterless fountain sits out front, surrounded by broken benches and the eerie sense of death. A single crow, naturally, lands on top of one of the church's spokes, cawing loudly to announce my presence.

Whispers drift to me on a ghostly breeze, although when I hunt for the source, no one is there. Shadows loom behind boarded-up store fronts and cracks in curtains. I shudder with unease, the hairs on the back of my neck on high alert.

Calling for the purple glow to surround my hands, since my power responds so much easier in alternative astral planes, movement shifts to my right. The door of a tall town house flies open, smacking against the wooden railing as a figure steps out. The generous curves of her body tell me straight away she's a female, regardless of the bulky fatigues and baggy black vest hanging from her frame. Two strips of bullets criss-cross over her chest, her luscious brown waves shift around a slender face which is blocked by the machine gun pointing in my direction. At her back, three shadows step forward, their shoulders crammed as they wriggle out of the doorframe.

"State your name," the female orders in a strangely familiar voice. Although, the icy tone cuts through me like a whip and the orbs in my hands grow on instinct.

"Hoax," I reply steadily. I could just shift out of here but I'm intrigued as to where I've ended up. Slowly walking forward on long legs ending in a pair of killer biker boots, the woman descends the steps and lowers her LMG. Chocolate brown eyes peer at me curiously, her blemish-free face tilting slightly. There's recognition in her features, but also confusion. Lowering her gun completely, she pushes her finger and thumb into her mouth and whistles sharply.

"He's a mute!" she shouts, and bodies swarm into the square from all directions. Hair and eye colors from the entire color spectrum and beyond assault me, the mutterings of curiosity leaking through my ears. *Who is he? Where did he come from?* But there's only one girl that has my full attention. The one that appears to be running this show.

"Mania," I reach out to brush my hand through her brunette hair. "You haven't died yet."

"Excuse you?" she balks, jerking out of my touch. A scowl is etched into her eyebrows and the grip on her gun tightens. "The name's Mia and you'd be smart to keep your hands to yourself if you want to keep them." Gesturing her chin over her shoulder, I watch the men moving to catch up in keen interest. Pyro, Ghost and...myself. None of us have any tattoos, or the hauntedness of a tortured life. Instead, there's a steel edge to our gazes, a hard ridge to our defined muscles and gritty determination locked in our jawlines.

"You're all...Mutes," I breathe, peering at the sea of faces staring back at me. Some I recognize – Allergen, Roadrage, Stingray. Enzo with his ebony skin and dreads, pulling Claire and Tate into his sides.

Tate's vibrant purple eyes watch me closely and with a simple scrunch of her nose, the orbs in my hands die out.

"What else would we be?" the mirror image of myself asks. I fight the urge to roll my eyes, having seen enough versions of myself to last forever. Pyro's hair ignites with flame as his arm slides around Mania, or Mia as it turns out, his ability activating with the connection of their bond.

"Ha," I laugh bitterly under the scrutiny of stares, "where I come from, the streets are swarmed with humans. Not Mutes." A callous laugh erupts from Mania, followed by the rest of the crowd as they close in on me. Glints of weapons catch the light of the flickering streetlamp, every single Mute armed to the teeth. If there ever were humans in this world, it's not a huge mystery as to where they went. Over the mass of heads and past the church, a mountain of bones and skulls catches my eye. It stretches back as far as the eye can see and the same crow from before swoops over to take his place on top.

"That sounds like Hell," Ghost mutters through the laughter and Mania leans her head over onto his bicep.

"You have no idea," I agree. In whatever flipped reality this is, it's Ghost and Pyro who are standing with nothing but seriousness lacing his expressions, and me who's hanging all over Mania like a love-sick puppy. A wide smile is spread across my mirrored face while Pyro glares on with a deranged hint to his fiery red eyes. This Pyro I don't know. This one looks like he'd shoot me in the face for sport and skin me into a rug or some shit. At least my other self seems impassive as ever. Suppose that's just my M.O.

"Everyone about your business. There's nothing to see here." Mania snaps after the laughter has died down. Obeying her order, the Mutes slink back to their hideouts, more than a few dragging their weapons behind them in disappointment. Slinking out of Pyro's hold, she closes the distance between us and reaches up to tussle my indigo hair. I can't hide my appreciative shiver, having waited far too long to feel her touch again. "Tell me, what else is different in your world?"

"Everything," I breathe, moving my head so her hand falls onto my cheek and briefly closing my eyes. "The three of you are trapped in a maze of torture, set up by a human that experiments on and kills

Mutes for fun." A frown pinches my eyebrows, yet I want to selfishly revel in this moment for a little while longer. Mania's fingers drop to my neck, curving around my collarbone and across the circuits of my tattoos. She follows the wires with her fingertips, lightly sparking their hardwiring from the inside. My power responds, carving purple tendrils everywhere she touches.

"The three of us?" she asks in a small voice, as fascinated by the glowing wires among the ink as I am.

"I'm dead," I sigh. "I've been stuck watching from the other side. Trying to help when I can…but I'm useless."

"Doesn't sound like you're useless to me. Nice to know I have a guardian angel watching over me, in whatever realm you come from." I don't bother correcting her about astral planes and whatever shit Asher told me. For all I know, I could be hallucinating or in a death coma. "Well you'd better get back to it. This fine ass isn't going to watch itself."

"No it's not," the other Hoax agrees, his eyes dropping. I can only imagine what slice of heaven it is to hide away with Mania in a town house, uninterrupted by the hunt of humans or trials of tyrants. Swallowing the wash of jealousy, I'm already vowing to myself I can never come back here. No matter how tough it is to be the outsider looking in, this isn't my Mania. She's theirs. As if following my train of thought, the three males opposite nod their heads and turn to leave.

"But let me give you something before you go. Maybe it'll help," Mania says. Sliding her hand around the back of my neck, she tiptoes to push her lips against mine. My deadened heart skips a beat in my chest, the feel of her pressed against me opening a whole bag of carvings I've kept under wraps. The sweetest torture. A beautiful suffering I allow myself to indulge in this once. The warm caress of her mouth over mine is enough to bring me to my knees, if I couldn't feel the eyes of her men staring from the house steps. I have to uphold appearances.

Trailing my hand down her arm, I dislodge the gun from her grasp and tilt to drop it on the floor. Then my hands grab her ass and I hoist her up against my body, craving the feel of her core against my growing length. It's been too long to be gentle. Too hard watching her grow closer to others when I can feel the void between us growing deeper. Delving into our kiss, my tongue skates over hers, coaxing her to take me in any way she likes. Hands grip, fingernails scratch. The heat between us rockets to a fever pitch and I couldn't give a fuck who's watching. Drawing her over my rigid shaft, her breasts press into my chest and for a second I still at the feel of our hearts beating in unison.

Sinking her teeth into my bottom lip, Mania leaves no room for regret. No chance of a missed opportunity. She leaves me breathless and yearning, but that'll have to be enough. For this lifetime at least. Resting my forehead against her, noting the crack that isn't permanently nestled into her skull. She's similar, but she's not mine. My Mania has seen the inside of Hell and sauntered out. She's guarded her heart so long, she doesn't even realize we've dug beneath the surface and buried ourselves into her soul.

Placing this version of her back onto her feet, Mania scoops down to pick up her gun as a being appears at the end of the street. Asher's face is contorted with rage, his borrowed specter glowing a lime green in his bloodied hand. Two guesses as to who won the prize on my bounty. Bending my head, I move my mouth to Mania's ear.

"Fancy doing me one more favor, beautiful?" She smirks in my direction, melting into my body like butter. Seems I'm not the only one who can't sense where the lines become too blurred between us. "Hold that asshole off for a while. I have a damsel in distress to return to." A harsh laugh croons from Mania's throat before she pushes her fingers into her mouth and whistles loudly again, this time in my ear.

"I don't care what dimension you're from; I'm no fucking damsel." She smacks my ass with a wink before screaming for her oncoming troops to attack Asher. Saluting the men on the porch, they return my gesture with a nod, not making any move to help the girl pledging a full-on war with a demon before them. And when her entire body ignites into a display of flame and rage, I can see why.

I make the active decision to avoid the real world for a little while longer. Going from a Mania that is ruling her world, to one that is being fucked by it isn't my idea of fun. Not when my power is volatile and unresponsive when I need it most. Instead, I head back to the place I should avoid, but figure while Asher is busy, it's my chance to find out more information on the mission that involves enslaving me to the Devil. Words I never thought I'd need to contemplate but nothing surprises me anymore. In the least, betrayal.

Appearing in the place I last stood, I first notice the lack of Azella's presence, and then the horde of demons who weren't here before. Around a dozen males, in both human and half-animal form, gathering around a patch burnt into the already charred grass. It looks suspiciously like a body and given the lack of Mantus, I would make the fair assumption this is where he last laid. The demons stand with their eyes closed, chanting together as a crunch draws my attention to behind me.

"You missed the best part," Hog-Face says around a mouthful of food. He's still sitting on a checked picnic blanket, stuffing his face with an array of wrappers littered around him. Having kicked off his boots, his knobbly feet are crossed, his toes wriggling back and forth.

It all comes back to me then and I start fisting my hands by my sides, staring over at the line of prisoners diverting in a wide arc to avoid the demons standing in their usual queueing spot. I can't become one of them. Fun as it was to help Asher drag a few souls down here that once, I can't be weighted with the responsibility of reaping souls. Especially when I come across those I don't believe deserve it – like Mutes.

"Why didn't he just tell me of his intentions?" I ask, twisting my head towards Hog-Face. "Asher. Why did he try to trick me into becoming a demon instead of just being upfront?" Hog-Face shrugs, wiping off his crumby hands on his dark slacks.

"My guess - he knew you wouldn't come easy. And it's much easier for someone to come easy." I stare at him blandly and purse my lips.

"How insightful," I remark. He holds up a half greasy hoof and I take it, dragging him up to his feet. Clicking his fingers the blanket disappears and a rumble rocks through the ground. A spear of red and orange light pierces the cloud-ridden sky, blasting into the ground where the blanket just lay. "Little excessive, don't you think?"

"Err," Hog-Face pulls me a few steps back, our hands still connected. "That's not me." I pull out of his greasy grip, marveling the blaze. The light is held in a perfect cylinder, not a wisp out of place. Through the inferno of what seems like fire, a figure of royal blue is lowered slowly. Just like the woman dancing inside Pyro's flames, her hair shifts easily. Slender arms hang loosely by her sides, her figure creating the perfect form. Despite the lack of features, there's something eerily similar about her and I find myself drawn forwards. Hog-Face tries to hold me back, telling me to steer clear but it's useless. I'm entrapped in a snare of curiosity. I need to know who it is.

Lifting a hand, my fingers graze the light and to my surprise, it doesn't burn. Not a lick of heat dances across my skin. Stepping inside, losing sight of anyone or anything else, my heart beats one solid thump in my chest. My subconscious knew what to expect, but the implications of being right hasn't settled in yet. I step into her blue-encased body, my hands settling on her hips and the instant I do, it's as if someone turned off the light switch. The orange glow cuts out, exposing us to the underworld. She collapses in my arms, the blue hue fading from her lifeless body in the darkness. I drop to my knees, cradling her. Hugging her to me so tight in the ways I've been dreaming, but not like this. Never like this.

"She's never been delivered to us that way before," Asher's grave voice sounds and I gasp as if I've been kneed in the gut.

"What does that even mean?!" I shout back, ignoring the attention of the male demons ambling over to get a closer look. I want to lash out, to knock them all on their asses but my hands won't release Mania's beautiful body for shit. The red portion of her hair trickles over my arms like blood, the blackened ends reuniting with the charred grass like it's a part of her. Hell, is a part of her. Dark lashes fan her purely white cheeks, the tattoos against her skin seeming brighter. Each skull stares out as if representing the lives she's lived but this is the one that matters. This is the one where she found love.

"I suspect it's her final visit. The one she doesn't return from," I hear Asher's sigh and a growl is torn from me.

"Get fucked," I spit, hugging her closer to me. Asher can't hunt me through the planes, can't *anger* me with his lies, and then have the gall to sound concerned for Mania. Drawing on the power inside, I strain with the effort to create a simple purple glow around my hands. Gritting my jaw, I try again and again, begging for the energy to answer my call this one damn time. The grass crunches as Asher crouches in my peripheral vision, his hand landing on my shoulder.

"It's no use," he mutters quietly. Shaking my head, I refuse to believe him and continue to try. To fight against myself. "Your power won't work because you never really had any. It was me, Hoax – I was gifting you hints of power to show you what it'd feel like."

"No...no. I used it by myself when you weren't there. Unless..."

"I was always there," he nods heavily. Pure rage courses through me that he's pretending to care now. Hanging his head in remorse, he tries to reach out a hand to stroke Mania's hair and I whip her away. If I felt comfortable putting her down, I'd have snapped his fucking neck already. I'm not a fighter, and apparently I have no power of my own, but I vow this demon will join Mantus' side, becoming nothing more than an outline in the grass. Hog-Face rounds my front, intent on taking her from me and that's when the truth settles in. I'm about to lose her, forever.

Throwing my head back, I howl. Scream and cry damn it, with every ounce of pain and agonizing misery consuming me. Even the other demons step back through the haze of my tears, giving me space while the clinking of the prisoner's shackles shift uncomfortably. Attempting to relieve me of her again, I snarl at Hog-Face's hand, daring him to come closer. No one touches her. She's not a soul to be reaped, not yet. And all the while, Asher hovers over my shoulder like a condescending fuck, his hand never leaving my shoulder.

"It's going to be okay, brother," he murmurs and despite my little-bitch sobbing, a mechanical laugh is drawn from my lips.

"I'm going to fucking destroy you," I promise him. "They won't even be able to find your remains to chant over."

"It won't seem like it now, or for a long time yet, but I was trying to do what was best for you. Living between worlds is a fate worse than death." Asher's words are laced with experience but now's not the time to have a cuddle puddle. Shrugging him off, I finally rise to my feet and carefully place Mania into Hog-Face's sturdy arms.

"Don't move a muscle," I threaten with a glare. Then, I twist my body and provide a formal meeting between Asher's jaw and my boot. He doesn't budge, not even when I do it again and blood oozes from the split in his lip. Simply sits there, looking up at me. Kicking him in the chest, he's minorly dislodged from his crouch but I don't get any of the reward I'm hunting for. Just an impassive stare and slightly cocked eyebrow until he slowly stands. The next time I move, Asher simply raises his hand and renders me frozen in place.

"You didn't do this for me," I manage to grit out of an unmoving mouth. "You did it for you. To get back in the Devil's good books." Nodding, Asher releases me from his hold. I ignore the puppy dog feature to his golden eyes, or how the lava coursing through the scarred side of his face dims as if it's cooling.

"You're right," he half shrugs. "But you surpassed my expectations. I spent half my time trying to pull back the power I unleashed in you. Even then, you managed to wield whatever tendrils were left in there." He prods a finger into my chest, which is still heaving but I don't react. I figure it's my time to listen. "You'd make a cracking demon, and I reckon the possibilities would be endless." Over the top of his spectacles that do nothing to hide the solid gold of his irises, he flicks a look in Mania's direction. Hog-Face balks, heavy breaths puffing from his tusked mouth. His snout trembles and on closer inspection, he's holding Mania with the upmost care his gnarled fingers can manage.

"If I do this, will I be able to save her?" I frown, clenching my fists hard enough to bleed from my own nails.

"I can't promise either way. It's never been done before, and not for lack of trying," Asher looks away, a pained pinch of misery taking over his face. "But you continue to break the laws of life and death, defying the natural order. It's our only shot." I don't miss the way he says ours as if he cares what happens to Mania. Scratching a hand over his smoking beard, Asher assesses me carefully, waiting for my next move. My final decision.

Peering over his shoulder, I weigh my options up on the rolling gray clouds in the distance. But what options are there? Remain living between worlds until Pyro's eternal flame releases me from our tie, watching my brothers mourn and unable to see Mania again until we all pass through the gates. Who knows what we'll find when we do. Or I become a demon, enslaved to the Devil himself. Even if I fail in saving her, I'd get to be with Mania, but at what cost to my soul.

So in conclusion, there really is no other option. This is my only chance to save Mania. Slumping my shoulders, I turn to press my lips to the crack in her forehead and send her a silent vow. Hold on Sweetheart, I'm coming for you.

A weighty robe is placed over my shoulders and I ask again if we can hurry this the fuck up. Mania is still out cold, which doesn't bode well for her spirit. Whether on her last life or not, she should have at least woken up by now to join the other prisoners. Azella purses her lips, slicking down my wild hair like the mother I never had.

"Stop worrying. If you manage to revive her, barely any time will have passed up top." Pulling the robe further over my collar bone, she brushes her clawed fingers over the buttons of a black shirt she dressed me in while I stood around like a lemon, staring into space.

"And if I don't?" I catch Azella's green eyes and plead with her to ease my conscience.

"Then you can hold her hand through the Hellfire and lead her to her cell." I know she meant to be comforting, but her words only deepen the guilt swirling in my gut. Nodding her horns at me to gesture I'm as ready as I'll ever be, we exit the chamber carved into the outside wall of Hell. It looks like a temporary holding cell with a grate that can slide downwards over the threshold if needed.

Stepping out in the ritual clothing Asher provided me with, I see a mass of demons waiting just inside of the iron gates. The very ones

I've been determined not to step through. Hog-Face is still cradling Mania to his chest, the only male I was at ease holding her. Despite his rough-around-the-edges and blocky appearance, he's taking the utmost care in holding her while she sleeps. Or...remains dead until further notice.

Inhaling deeply, I step over the threshold, a tremor of nerves finding me through my steely posture. I refuse to show weakness in front of those who have passed this ceremony, even as the fires through the archways roar to the sky, preparing to seal my fate. Closing in behind me, the demons hold the prisoners back, allowing me a short space of time but the queue is already becoming backed up as far as I can see.

"Remember my instruction. Step into the fires and repeat these words," Asher pushes a scrunched up note with a Latin incantation scribbled on. I wriggle my nose, figuring the paper will burn the instant I walk in the fires but I don't waste any more time in doing so. Passing beneath the unconnected stone archways, I briefly wonder if there was ever the rest of the structure to complete it. The fires part, anticipating my entry before I'm ready for it, but here goes nothing.

Fire softly burns at my heels, not enough to melt the leather of my boots but I feel it. The heat is gentle, like a caress lulling me into a false sense of security. Once fully inside, I manage to catch one last glimpse of Azella's eyes filled with concern before the veil closes behind me and I'm trapped. The robe on my back ignites, burning away to ash that trickles into the fires, beginning the ritual. Flames swirl, licking the backs of my legs until I am swept into a tornado of destruction. My skin becomes warped, rippling like the sea as I spot the piece of paper intact in my hand.

"Grata mihi, ignis. Paratus sum fieri daemon," I try to say with confidence. Mostly I just fuck up the words but on the third and fourth time, it seems to roll off the tongue a little easier. When nothing happens, I fear I've done it wrong but then a streak of black slices through the ombre red to orange. It cages me, appearing anywhere I look and damn all my masculinity, I take a step back. But no, this is for Mania. Either I'm reaped or I become the reaper, backing out isn't an option.

Swirling faster, the streaks fuse into one, crackling like a web and solidifying the fires into a clay cavern I can't escape. When they have nowhere else to go, the webs embed themselves into my skin. Covering me so thickly, my tattoos are no longer visible. Then, they start to pull. Dragging me down to the ground, covering my mouth when I try to scream.

Swallowing me whole, I drag my fingernails across the Earth, crawling to stay above ground. The black webs on my arms shift into runes that begin to shine with the burning embers of Hellfire. A similar glow emanates from my chest but I don't look down to see what demonic scripture is printed there. Instead, my attention is drawn high above as I literally hang in the balance. The fires contort into an oval that suddenly reveals itself as a glowing eye. The mark of the demon, as I've seen imprinted on the others. Prying my mouth open between the blackened web, I manage to croak out the Latin spell one last time and the eye descends, plunging into my body.

Spat out by the Earth, I crash onto the ground, gasping and writhing from the uncomfortable feeling inside. It ravishes every last corner of my being, intruding on my body with its hollowness. An entity completely void of life. Because that's what I am not. Not just dead, but soulless. With that final understanding, the *thing* inside me settles. Becoming one with me. The fires settle back to their usual roar, the curtain prying open for me to army crawl out of. Asher is there in a flash, helping me to my feet and brushing a thumb over my neck. I don't need to see it to know that's where my demon mark is. A sizzle between my flesh, a tantalizing burn of deathly promise. The other runes have disappeared and I spare no time thinking about how wrong that ceremony for one could have just gone.

Rushing forward on numb feet, I lightly take Mania into my arms as her eyes begin to open. Thanking Hog-Face, I take her into the exterior chamber, needing space from the staring eyes. Luckily, Asher takes the hint and yells for everyone to fuck off, while Azella remains hovering not too far away.

"Where-where am I?" Mania asks from the clutch of my embrace. I grip her tightly, unable to hide the shiver raking through my spine. "Hoax? What's happening?" I bury my face into her neck, taking a selfish moment to relish in the feel of her against me. Finally. My lips brush her collar bone and then I'm back on task.

"I'm going to break you free," I whisper, kissing her crack-ridden forehead. "I'm going to fix your eternal flame with Pyro." I don't know where the thought comes from but as the words leave my mouth, it all makes sense. She wouldn't still be down here if her bond to Pyro was still intact, and since I have the flames both tied to my spirit and melded into my physical body, there has to be a way *I* can activate them.

Pressing a hand to her chest, I close my eyes. Hunting. Searching for the demon powers that have nothing to do with Asher's aid. The response to my call is a stroke of pleasure beneath my skin. A dark, twisted enchantment I lean into, biting back the groan it sweeps through me. I'm not naïve, once unleashed this power will coax me in deeper until I'm consumed. Infected with the rush. Tainted with its strength.

In my mind's eye, a sphere of fire ignites. Fierce in appearance but comforting in the loving warmth that spreads through me. Pyro's eternal flame. I surge my being into it, adding fuel to his fires with purple gasoline. The more I integrate myself inside, the larger it grows and a harsh gasp is torn from Mania.

"You feel that, baby?" I ask through my daze. "You see that? It's all for you. Join me." Spreading my fingers wider over her chest, I lift her diaphragm in time with the pulse at the side of my neck. Forcing her heart to beat, drawing the blood through her veins like a tide rolling in and out. A black skull appears inside the fiery sphere behind my eyelids and I know she's arrived. She's found a way in.

Black smoke pours from the skull's eyes, and her scream of determination howls inside my own ears. The purple energy I'm adding divides into wires. Sparking electrical wires that link to one adjoining circuit around the sphere. The instant the fireball morphs into the shape of a heart, I know the connection between the four of us is complete and Mania jerks upright in my arms. Our eyes lock at the same time our lips do, a rogue tear falling between us on her cold cheek.

"We need to get you out of here," I murmur. Trying to teleport, I groan in frustration when we don't budge. Mania's lips are too busy covering me in the kisses we've been deprived of, the ones I'd happily lose myself in anywhere else but here. A sudden rumble rocks the ground and I straighten, bracing myself when Asher steps into the doorway. The sky beyond him crackles with a fork of lightning flashing in the distance, an impending storm rolling this way.

"You're upsetting the balance. She cannot fight her fate. It's too late." I growl at Asher when he reaches for her, pushing one foot in front of the other to barge past him. Like she's tied to a bungee rope, the instant I leave the chamber, Mania begins to be pulled towards the iron gates. The fires inside are crackling, spitting and hissing. Churning into a blue hue, I can practically feel her name being called in the fire's roars. Mania doesn't respond, the wetness of her tears causing her cheek to slide against my chest. I can feel in her posture she's given up but that doesn't mean I will.

"This isn't fate. It's fucking..." I growl, not having the words. "I'm stuck between two worlds because of some asshole holding my consciousness on a flash drive. Mania doesn't deserve this fate any more than I do. You were a Mute once Asher, and like us you weren't given a chance. Give her a fucking chance to finally be happy for once."

Another fork of lightning divides the sky up ahead, the flash blindingly bright and in its wake, a single spear of light is left. One slip of sunshine among the endless dark clouds and my eyes widen. That's it, it has to be. Her way out.

Clutching her tightly, I twist Mania out of the pull trying to drag her into the gates of Hell and take a labored step forward. She presses into me now, the understanding dawning. The long line of prisoners reach for us, shackled by their chains and compliantly walking toward their destiny. Nails claw at my arms, trying to drag Mania towards their clutches but I turn my back on them too. She's not theirs. She doesn't belong here. The crisp, charred grass breaks beneath my boots, the powerful pull causing me to skid backwards.

"No!" I bellow to the sky. "You can't have her!" Even with the roared call of her fate blazing at my back, I won't let those fires take Mania from me. I won't watch her from the other side of a cell any more than I've despised watching from the other side of the void. Especially when I've come this far.

Each footstep becomes heavy but I refuse to stop, the slip of light growing painfully closer. A pair of hands pressed against my back, then another and when I prepare myself to fight them off, I feel their push of encouragement. Asher's golden eyes and Azella's green ones give me steely looks of determination over my shoulder and together, the three of us fight against Hell's pull. Step, heave, step, heave. Together in unison, we move until the light is almost upon us and Mania curls up in against my chest.

"I can't lose you again," she whimpers and I press my cheek against her hair.

"You've never lost me. I've been with you, and I always will be." Her blood-red eyes find mine, her perfect porcelain face too much to bear. Skating my thumb over her lips, she presses a kiss there and the crack of thunder behind tells me we're out of time. "I love you, for eternity," I say, and throw her into the slip of light.

"Mania!" Pyro's voice whips through the air before a vine does the same, closing over his mouth. The depressing outer face of Afterlife Asylum looms over me, my hopes of an easy escape dashed once more. If it's not a labyrinth Mania is trying to navigate, it's another cruel turn of events at Christopher's hand. She stands there, in all her living glory, the image of rage and her red eyes swirling with the promise of death. All of which is currently centered on a speaker with Christopher's mocking laughter rolling out.

Also trapped against the wall by vines, Mania's shoulders heave, smoke billows from her mouth like that of a dragon. I tilt my head curiously when the aroma of burning fills my lungs. I pause mid-inhale, looking down at myself. Canvas shoes and cargo pants cover my lower half and the shirt I was wearing has vanished. A thick metal chain is wrapped around my wrists, the end trailing into the grass and forgotten about. Realizing I can feel their heavy weight, that I can smell the smoke and feel the lick of a breeze, my heart judders in my chest. My very real, beating heart. I'm…alive.

Ghost attends to freeing Mania from her confines while I pat myself down. The chains clink and despite myself, a small smile hooks up the side of my mouth. Hardly the happy ending I was hoping for but it's a start. A figure catches my attention from the shadow of the bleachers, Asher's face glowing as the lava bubbles beneath his cheek. Raising one brow of his spectacles, he nods and vanishes with a tap of his specter. Reaching up dully, my fingers drag over the warmth of the symbol on my neck. The demon mark.

So while Ghost kisses Mania and murmurs in her ear, while Pyro is still pinned to the wall of the asylum and a green gas begins to hiss from the drain at their feet, I merely stand here. Alive and keeping my distance, wondering how the hell I'm going to tell them I've sold myself to the Devil.

Thank you for reading book 2.5 in All My Pretty Psychos Series. I was so eager to give Hoax a voice and let his story come to life. This is a dark paranormal reverse harem romance which will ultimately (eventually) have a HEA at the end of the trilogy so hang in there! Below you'll find the blurb for the third and final book in this series – Reign of Chaos.

If you haven't read any other series' by me yet, you have to put I Love Candy on your TBR! She's the twisted heroine you didn't know you needed and won't forget! Bye for now my literary lovers.

Reign of Chaos
All My Pretty Psychos Book Three
By Maddison Cole

Deprived beings bonded by the Eternal flame make the trickiest captives.
Divided. Disconnected. Yet stronger than ever. I don't need to see my men to feel them; the hum of their raw power simmering beneath the cuffs clamped around my wrists. Christopher may have us trapped

once more, his mocking laughter echoing around the walls of the asylum, but he's overlooked one simple fact. With my harem, I am fierce. Without them, I'm feral.

Dying is no longer an option. Hiding in Hell is a distant memory. A war has been waged upon the Mutes, and it's not just Christopher in my sights now. It's the entire human race. Whatever it takes, whatever I have to do, I will be free of these stone walls and the world of poverty beyond. If an uprising is needed to gain the Mutes equal rights, then I'm prepared to fight. For love has found me in the most unlikely of places, and Hell hath no fury like a mutant scorned.

Trigger warning: This novel is the third and final in a dark paranormal RH trilogy. Certain themes such as sex, self-harm, death and controversial beliefs are featured. However, those who always fall for the twisted, deranged villain and never question their own sanity about it, then come on in. The Afterlife Asylum is the place for you.

ACKNOWLEDGMENTS

Thank you for reading Hoax's Novella in the All My Pretty Psychos Series. I've had so much fun writing this book and giving Hoax his voice, and I really hop you enjoyed it just as much!

This is a dark reverse harem romance which will ultimately (eventually) have a HEA at the end of the trilogy, which means there's only one book to go. So, hang in there!

There are so many people who boost me on a daily basis, picking me up and giving me strength to continue when the words seem o evade me.

I want to say a big thanks as always to Sam, for being a great editor.

Emma, thanks again for making this book look just as great as the others.

Mr Cole and my gorgeous children - thank you for being so patient with me while I write, and for supporting me in this crazy journey.

To my amazing readers - thank you for loving my books and for devouring my words. You are the reasons I can keep doing what I love, and I'm forever grateful for that.

ABOUT MADDISON

Maddison is a married mum of two, and a serial daydreamer. As a huge fan of all romance tropes herself, it was time to pen the stories which consume her mind most hours of the day.

As a child, Maddison was a jet setter and has lived all over the world, only to return to the south east of England, where she is now happily settled. With a double award in applied arts and art history, Maddison is a creative with a dark passion for feisty females and spicy stories.

If you're a new reader to me – welcome to the mad house! Keep reading for my list of writes, and for up-to-date info, make sure you follow my socials! The reader's group is the best place for reveals, announcements, giveaways and more, and please never hesitate to reach out! I love hearing from readers.

Sign up to my newsletter here:
http://eepurl.com/hx3Zqr

Also, make sure to join my Facebook readers group, Cole's Reading Moles here:
www.facebook.com/colesreadingmoles

facebook.com/maddison.cole.314
instagram.com/maddison_cole_author
amazon.com/author/B086ZQ6SW4
bookbub.com/authors/maddison-cole
tiktok.com/@authormaddisoncole

ALL MY PRETTY PSYCHOS

Paranormal RH with ghosts and demons

Queen of Crazy

https://amzn.to/3O4biQt

Kings of Madness

https://amzn.to/3HzvBCY

Hoax: The Untold Story (novella)

https://amzn.to/3xAJhcA

Reign of Chaos

https://amzn.to/3b95PcI

I LOVE CANDY

Dark Humor RH - Completed

Findin' Candy (novella)

https://amzn.to/3bcueOp

Crushin' Candy

https://amzn.to/3n0TASf

Smashin' Candy

https://amzn.to/3Oniuai

Friggin' Candy

https://amzn.to/3QwlmUb

Candy - The Complete Collection

https://amzn.to/3LvatBu

.

THE WAR AT WAVERSEA

Basketball College MFM Menage - Completed

Perfectly Powerless

https://amzn.to/3OqHTQp

Handsomely Heartless

https://amzn.to/3tMoRfu

Beautifully Boundless

https://amzn.to/3MYiiNG

BOUND BY FATE

Vampire/Shifters Fated Mates Standalones